Evie Peach

St. Louis, 1857

⊶⊷

by Kathleen Duey

⊶⊷

Aladdin Paperbacks

For Richard For Ever

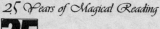

First Aladdin Paperbacks edition December 1997
Copyright © 1997 by Kathleen Duey

Aladdin Paperbacks
An imprint of Simon & Schuster
Children's Publishing Division
1230 Avenue of the Americas
New York, NY 10020

The text of this book was set in Fairfield Medium
Printed and bound in the United States of America
10 9 8 7 6 5 4 3 2

Library of Congress Cataloging-in-Publication Data
Duey, Kathleen.
Evie Peach, St. Louis, 1857 / Kathleen Duey. — 1st Aladdin
Paperbacks ed.
p.   cm. — (American diaries)
Summary: Emancipated by their owner's will, thirteen-year-old
Evie and her father struggle to gain Mama's freedom and to
make a home for themselves in the pre-Civil War South.
ISBN 0-689-81621-9 (pbk.)
1. Afro-Americans—Juvenile fiction. [1. Afro-Americans—
Fiction. 2. Slavery—Fiction.] I. Title. II. Series.
PZ7.D8694Ev   1997
[Fic]—dc21   97-35641
CIP   AC

Almost dawn. A steamboat whistle woke me. I can't sleep, so I have lit my candle stub and will write my promise-pages. Pa stayed up working the forge until almost midnight, but I know he'll be up early, too. I feel almost dizzy-headed. Today will be like a hundred Christmastimes all at once. After years of saving every cent, this is the day Pa and I will go to Marse James's farm to buy out Mama. Then we will go to the court-house to get her freedman paper and then we can come home! On our visit last Sunday, Pa said we could wait on the courthouse, but Mama said, "No, sir! I am tak-ing no chances on some slave trader selling me South because I haven't paid up my license!"

She gets so scared about all this that Pa has to hold both her hands still and kiss her forehead to calm her down. She says that Negroes starve once they are free. Papa tells her again about all the freedmen who own houses and businesses here in St. Louis—all the barbers and steamboat stewards like his friend Willis. Last night at supper Pa stretched up tall and turned to me while I was pulling the sweet potatoes out of the ashes.

"Marse William taught us to read and write, and

we have got to teach your mama," he said. "Even if she is scared to learn." I reminded him that reading could get us sold South—that Mama has a right to worry. He shook his head. He is sure the law will change.

I try to believe him. There are a lot of free blacks doing just fine. There are a lot who look poor and starved, too. But St. Louis is not like other places farther South. Nothing is as bad as the big plantations where the white folks don't even know all their own slaves and they sell off babies if they need more money that year. Missouri has mostly small farms. There's only the hemp farms out in Little Dixie that are big. Hemp is a killing crop, Pa says. Like cotton. It kills the folks who have to do the rough work, he means. Pa grew up doing fieldwork and broke hemp before Marse William bought him. He has long, ugly whip scars on his back.

Marse James's place is small. With Mama, Sam, and Fanny in the house and Kizzy, Jacob, and Horace out in the quarters, and Fanny's two sons— that's only eight slaves, all told, for all the hundred acres—and two of them are half-task boys who can only do half a man's work in a day. But they grow corn and oats there, not cotton or rope hemp. So they don't need a gang of slaves.

I was proud yesterday after Sunday school. I did a sum that no one else could do. I am getting better at figuring. Miss Ellia and Mr. Jenkins teach us real well. We can't have regular school because of the law, but we can sure study how many days Moses was in Egypt, or how many cubits in the ark. If I could, I'd go to the Reverend Meachum's boat-school, but Pa says no. It's too dangerous.

It will be hard to write two of these long old pages this morning. I am having trouble writing anything. The pen just wants to jump all over and fly out of my hand. I can barely believe that Mama, Pa, and I will be together in one house tonight. They have been married a year longer than I am old—thirteen years—and this is the first time they could ever live together. Marse William tried over and over to buy my mama from Marse James, but he wouldn't sell. Marse William bought me, though, when I was nine. I guess Marse James saw less money in me than Mama so he let me go. After all, Mama gets hired out for sewing all over, and Marse James earns a lot off that.

I am grateful to Marse William. He bought me when I was barely old enough to do any work for him at all. And if it wasn't for his will setting me and Pa free, Pa says he would have been white-headed before he saved up enough money to buy us all out. This way, we've only had to save two more years for Mama. Last night, Pa said the two years seem fly—past short now. Not for me. For me it seems like forever.

Marse James is so stingy, he's letting Mama's shoes wear on out on her poor feet and her dress get tattered up—because he knows she'll soon be gone. He is sorry he made the deal with Pa, I think.

I miss Marse William. I hope there's never more cholera. I am so thankful he manumitted us—otherwise we'd belong to his daughter now. Mistress Nancy used to lecture him about teaching us. Said he was crazy. Pa says white folks are afraid we will start reading Elijah Lovejoy and the other abolitionist papers, then start thinking and talking about something besides Sunday biscuits and church meeting. Besides them being afraid, I think they are just—

I don't remember now what I was about to write. I heard something and went to look out the window. It's the Maloney brothers. They are up to no good being out this early, you may be sure of that. Pa doesn't know about what they did to my speckled hen last week, and I'm not going to tell him. I have never told him any of it—how they follow me sometimes, teasing and pegging me with little rocks. I hate them. Poor Fiona, having brothers like that.

Now, I haven't quite filled these pages—but I am done! The sun is coming. It is going to be God's own most beautiful day. Today we go buy Mama out and bring her home!

CHAPTER ONE

Evie had been sitting humpy-backed over her book so long, she felt stiff. She stretched, arching her back. Then she leaned forward to set the old ledger book down, careful that the pages lay open flat so the ink would dry. Her light cotton shift stretched tight across her shoulders. Her clothes got small so quick lately. Pa kept saying she was growing fast.

The muted voices outside the window faded. Maybe they had gone away. Good. "I'll finish that page tonight," Evie whispered, looking upward toward heaven. Sometimes it felt like Marse William was looking down. She could imagine him smiling, his wrinkled old face crinkling up around his eyes and mouth. She had covered the cracked leather binding of the old ledger book he had given her with soft blue linen—scraps from Miss Ellia's last dress. Marse William didn't mind if she made his last gift a little prettier, more her own, she was sure.

Pa would say that was silly. Marse William wasn't looking down any more than God was. Pa had no religion at all. When she walked off to go to Sunday school, he always told her to be good, but he wouldn't come. Evie smiled. Mama would have them all going together. Mama loved church.

Evie corked the medicine bottle she used as an inkwell and put it and her pen into a wooden cheese box she had made into a writing box. It was almost time to ask Miss Ellia to get her more ink. Evie always said she used it to draw, which was partly true. And Miss Ellia never asked questions.

Evie blew at the ink, glancing toward the window. She had made flour-sack curtains. No one could see in, but she would feel better when her book was hidden.

Evie looked out the cracked window again, shivering. Somewhere off a block or so, a rooster crowed. Pa wouldn't let her keep a rooster. He said it would only give the neighbors a reason not to like them.

Evie shrugged. Besides Fiona, no one liked them anyway. Mr. Maloney made no secret of his dislike for all Negroes, and his wife was too busy trying to take care of her family to like anyone. The elderly couple on the corner stayed to themselves. Mr. Krieger next door couldn't speak much English. His wife spoke none at all. They both stared at Evie every time they saw her.

Evie blew on the ink again. The Kriegers were odd-looking. Their hair was so blond it was white, and their pink-yellow skin reminded her of a chicken's—right after its feathers were scalded and plucked.

The sound of boys' voices came through the window again. Evie frowned. Now the Maloney boys were arguing. The two oldest, Liam and Sean, always wrangled, each one trying to boss the younger three around. Paddy and Drew sometimes mutinied; the youngest, Terrence, never dared.

Terrence was barely eight, a skinny, pale boy who always had a runny nose. Evie felt sorry for him. All his brothers picked on him. But, then, they picked on everyone, including her. It was getting to where she went out the back door and down the alley when she left for Miss Ellia's and Mrs. Cummings's now. She had never told Pa how mean the boys were. It would only cause trouble.

Evie scrooched to the edge of her cot and swung her legs down, the corn husks and turkey feathers that filled her ticking mattress rustling beneath her. The web of cot ropes beneath the mattress creaked when she stood up.

Evie lifted her candle dish from the cot and held the flame close to the page she had just written. The ink was dull now. It had dried. She closed her book, then crouched to push it into the hiding place Pa had made beneath a loosened floor plank under her cot. She slid her writing box in on top and replaced the plank, running her palm across it to make sure it was set perfectly. Everything important they owned was in there. The money for Mama, their emancipation papers. Her father's freedman license was kept at the courthouse. He wasn't allowed to bring it home. But he had the receipt, to show he had posted his bond.

The voices outside rose, then fell. Were they fixing to play another mean trick? The poor speckled hen had almost died right where they tied her, way up in the maple tree. Evie had finally heard her weak clucking and climbed up to bring her down, but she hadn't laid an egg since. They only had four hens. That meant Pa couldn't have an extra egg for breakfast when he wanted it, and she had none to save for sale this week.

The two oldest Maloney boys were supposed to work, and the other three were supposed to go to the Catholic school. It seemed to Evie that they mostly roamed the streets looking for trouble.

Their voices seemed more distinct. Evie moved closer to the window, so she could see out slantwise through the little crack in the curtains. There. They were all in a bunch by the four spreading cottonwood trees that separated the yard and stable from Warren Street. They were talking, glancing between the thick, rough-barked trunks, keeping an eye on their own house. They *were* planning something.

Uneasy, angry that the Maloneys had any part in Mama's day, Evie pulled on her drawers, then her chemise, tugging the drawstring waist snug. Then she slid her dress over her head, straightening the sturdy blue cloth across her shoulders. Mama had made it like iron, with triple stitching. She knew how hard Evie was on clothes.

Evie tiptoed to her door, turned the crooked brass handle, and eased it open. The main room was pretty dim. Pa was still asleep. He had worked late to finish repairing the plowshare that belonged to Marse Halley, an old neighbor. His place was west of Marse William's and Marse James's.

Mr. Halley, Evie reminded herself. *Mr. Halley.* Marse James and Marse William had been her masters, but Mr. Halley hadn't. And now she didn't have a master at all. Pa thought all the people would set their slaves free in time. He always said there were too many fair-minded folks for slavery to go on forever.

But there were plenty of ignorant, mean-hearted folks, too, Evie thought. There were slaves down at Lynch's every day, some of them caught-up runaways, trying to make it to Illinois and free soil. All of them waiting with sick spirits and pounding hearts. A bad master meant misery, but if you ran away from that misery, it just got worse.

Evie hesitated, listening to Pa's even, deep breathing, then she opened the door. Pa was tall and wide both. His cot barely held him. He had made a new bed for him and Mama. It was standing upended against the wall, its rope mesh tight and newly stretched. Pa said he wouldn't use it until Mama came. Evie knew he had wanted to get a new moss mattress made, too, but he hadn't been able to. They would have to use his old one across the top and folded blankets across the bottom. Evie heard her father pull in a deep breath, then let it out in little snores. His blanket was up over his head. Shivering, she crossed the cool plank floor.

The main room was L-shaped, so it was really like having two rooms. Evie made it past her father's cot without him stirring. She went around the corner into the kitchen and stood against the rough plaster wall.

The hearth was full of powdery gray ash. Maybe someday they would have a cookstove, Evie thought as she listened for the Maloney boys' voices. Once Mama was home with them they could all start to save for a cookstove. Maybe someday they could even buy this house. Pa's friend had bought his. And he had been free only four years longer than Pa.

"Pssst!"

The whispery hissing sound came from just outside the front door. Evie heard a quick scuffle of footsteps. She stood on her toes to see out the narrow, cloudy window into the yard. The Maloney boys were probably past talking about whatever they meant to do.

Evie put her hand on the door latch and eased it upward. Maybe she could get where they couldn't see her and toss a few pebbles to make them think Pa was up and about this early. That might scare them off.

Evie opened the door a crack and peeked out. She couldn't hear voices at all now. For a few seconds, everything was silent, and she began to hope they would just go home.

Then, Evie heard someone whispering. They absolutely were doing something they shouldn't be. She opened the door another few inches and slid through the narrow opening onto the porch.

It was a little lighter outside than she had thought. She ducked behind the honeysuckle vine. In the same instant the sweet smell of the blossoms engulfed her, she realized that the Maloneys were just on the other side of the trellis.

CHAPTER TWO

Evie squeezed herself smaller, sinking cross-legged to the porch planks. She leaned forward until she spotted a gap in the heavy tangle of vines big enough to see through. The Maloney brothers were standing under the maple tree, facing each other like ducks around a torn corn bag. They were talking, their words tumbling one over the next, so she couldn't understand.

"Not the chickens again," Liam, the oldest, said. There were nods of agreement all around the circle. One of the middle brothers, either Paddy or Drew, lifted his head, only his silhouette visible against the lightening sky. "The horses this time?"

Evie felt her stomach tighten. If they went out to the stable, she would almost have to get her father up. His forge and workshop were out there. If the Maloneys hurt either of the mares with their fool-ishment, Pa wouldn't be able to deliver the repaired plows, heavy andirons, cookstove pedestals, and everything else he made. Lucky and Ginger were both old, trusting, and gentle. If Liam caused either one of them harm . . . Evie clenched her fists. She hated the Maloneys.

"We could just turn them out of their stalls," one of the boys whispered harshly.

"Naw," one of his brothers disagreed. "Then they won't know anyone did it. They'll just think they forgot to close the stall gates."

Framed by the little opening in the vines, Evie could see Liam's sharp, pale face, half turned away from her. "We could burn the whole place down. That would get them out of here. Father says that'd be the best thing everywhere. If they all went back to Africa there'd be more jobs, more money, more food—more of everything for us. They should never have come here anyway."

Evie tilted her head, listening hard, trembling with rage. Her grandmother had not *come* here from Africa. She had been *brought*.

"Mr. Simms says the Kriegers should go back to the Faderland, too," one of the younger boys said. Evie couldn't see which. "And us to Ireland."

Liam laughed quietly. "Simms is a Nativist, Pa says. That's stupid talk, us going back. We was starving in Ireland. I remember it."

"I do, too, Liam, barely. Mother says—"

"You talk too much," Liam hissed, and Evie could hear the others titter nervously.

"What about the horses?" That was Sean, impatient. Liam had been playing leader too long.

"I say we let them out," Liam said slowly. "But we have to leave a sign—something that says we want them to go back to Liberia."

"What's Liberia?"

Evie saw Terrence lift his head and she wondered if he ever would learn. Liam laughed softly again, his lips curled with contempt. "That's Africa. Liberia's the same as Africa. They want to make a colony for the Negroes there."

Liam stepped back out of Evie's view, and she bit thoughtfully at her lower lip and stilled her breathing, as she waited. She had heard of the colony in Liberia. Pa said more folks were thinking about it now that Dred Scott's court case had failed. The highest court in America had said that colored people couldn't be citizens, no matter what. So why stay once they were free?

Evie looked up at the sky. It was almost light. She shifted a little on the planks, pulling her knees up nervously. She leaned forward, staring through the little hole in the vine. After another moment, she stood up quietly. They had moved. Had Liam led them somewhere with a noiseless gesture?

"Come on!"

This was a harsh whisper from the other side of the yard, followed by a scuffle of feet. Evie risked a step forward, peering around the end of the trellis. She saw them filing down the path. Terrence giggled and Sean hissed at him, one finger raised to his lips. They walked single file down the row of dusty cottonwood trees, then bunched up again in front of the stable door. Evie watched. She glanced at the front door. If she woke her father—it was impossible to tell what might happen. Mr. Maloney could cause a world of trouble.

Nervous, Evie waited. The stable door was standing halfway open, and there was not a single Maloney brother in sight. Evie curled her bare toes, worried. Liam's voice came from inside the stable, low and urgent. Evie stepped off the porch. She ran, light-footed, toward the stable.

As she got close, Evie heard Lucky neigh uneasily. She sprinted to the door and shoved it closed. She dropped the heavy lock bar in place and jumped back, as though the Maloney boys could somehow come flying through the planks and attack her. She shifted her weight from one foot to the other, a nervous dance on the dusty path as she listened to the boys' voices from inside the stable.

"Open the door, Terrence, you brainless fool!"

"I didn't close it!"

"Well, then, who did? Whoever is closest, open it back up. It's too dark in here."

Evie saw the door move a little and knew someone was pushing on it from the inside. The lock bar would hold no matter what they did. But what now? Evie stared at the stable as if she had never seen it before. Was there another way out? There were no windows, only the high slatted vents. It was old— probably from the days when stock needed protection, before the city had grown this far north. It was solid, like a farm stable, strong and tight against foxes, wolves, coyotes. Her father had built his forge alongside it, but he hadn't made a door connecting the two. The Maloneys were not going to escape.

"Someone's barred it from outside!"

This astonished statement came from Sean, Evie was sure.

"Who did it?" Liam demanded in a hoarse whisper.

"How should I know?" Sean rasped back.

The words were clear as anything. They had to be standing right against the door.

"Maybe it was a ghost." This was Terrence's nervous attempt at making a joke, Evie realized. But after he said it, they all fell silent. Evie thought about Fiona with her constant prayers and lucky sayings and charms. An idea began to form in her mind.

Evie approached the door, staying to one side in case there were tiny cracks between the planks through which the boys could see her. For this to work, they would have to be convinced they were alone.

"Ooooooooohhhhhh," Evie moaned, so quietly she could barely hear herself. Then she made the sound again, just a little louder.

"What was that?" someone whispered inside the stable.

"OOOOOOOOOOoooooooooohhhhhhhhh," Evie responded, again raising her voice just a little. She made the sound eerie, like wind in a graveyard. Then she glanced back at the house. There was no sign that her father was up.

"Who's . . . who's out there?"

It was Liam's voice now, and Evie grinned at the little tremor in it. "Ooooooooooooooohhhhh," she sang back at him, putting all the misery of the world into the sound. She scratched lightly at the wood with her fingernails.

"Let's just go home and never mind the horses," Evie heard Terrence whine. Liam shushed him instantly.

"Is there another way out?" This was Sean. He sounded less scared than Terrence had, but not much. One of the boys gasped.

"I felt something touch my cheek."

"Probably a cobweb, you fool." Liam was trying to sound calm, but his voice was ragged.

Evie broke a slender branch from one of the cottonwoods. Stretching up onto her tiptoes, she rubbed it on the stable wall beside the door. It squeaked against the smooth wood. There were more gasps from inside. Evie raced to the back of the stable and thumped on the wall, once up as high as she could reach, then twice down low. The hay was stacked against this wall, and she was pretty sure the thumps would sound strange and muted from inside the stable. She ran back, going as fast as she could without making any noise.

She leaned close to the door again in time to hear Liam's shaking voice: "If the old man finds us like this, he'll—"

"Father at his worst isn't as bad as a ghost, Liam," Sean interrupted. "We should all start screaming. Then someone would come."

"Nooooo," Evie rasped, her face close to the wall beside the door. She scratched her nails into the wood again, making strange, crawly rhythms. Finally, without making a sound, she lifted the lock bar upward, then whirled to lay it silently on the ground. Then she moaned once more before turning to run around to the far side of the stable again.

Evie thudded her shoulder into the planks. Then

she moaned quietly. Another thump, then she paused, trying to hear above her racing heart. She thumped the wood once more, her fist closed. Then she began a high-pitched wailing, half breath, half voice.

"Oh, dear Lord." That was Sean's voice.

"Sean? Help me break the door down. We have to get out of here!" This was Liam. He sounded desperate. Evie moaned. It sounded like they were bumping into each other. She ran from the back of the stable, dashing to one of the tall cottonwoods along the street. Climbing fast, she shinned up the rough-barked trunk, not stopping until the thick branches concealed her.

Her breath heaving, her legs trembling, Evie waited. She couldn't see the stable door from her perch, but she could see a little section of Warren Street. "Hey, it's open," she heard Liam shout. Within seconds, the Maloney brothers were running back across the dusty street, strung out in a line with Terrence bringing up the rear. White-faced and wide-eyed, he kept glancing back toward the stable.

Evie waited until she was sure they were gone. Then she climbed down, dropping onto the soft ground. Cautiously, she made her way back up the path. Lucky and Ginger whickered a greeting as she came in the door. She gave them each a little hay, then went out, dropping the lock bar into place. Then she ran for the house.

CHAPTER THREE

Evie lay on her bed, listening, watching the sky lighten outside the window. Her father was stirring now. She could hear the ropes beneath his mattress creaking as he turned over, then back. Just as the sun broke free of the horizon, Evie heard him yawn, a big, noisy, stretchy yawn like always. Then she heard his footsteps on the plank floor.

"Evie? You awake?"

"Yes!" she answered. "I'm up, Pa."

"You remember what day this is?"

"I'm shaking and shivering over what day this is."

She heard him laugh. "Then get your pretty self dressed. Let's get started on breakfast. I'm not that hungry, but we'd best eat before we leave. Marse James won't be happy to see us too early anyway."

"I'm coming, Pa," Evie said, not about to tell him that she was already dressed. She went to the window and pulled the soft cotton curtain aside to look across the street. The Maloney brothers were nowhere to be seen now. She hadn't heard them even once in the whole last hour. Evie smiled, remembering once more how scared they had sounded. As she watched, the front door of the Maloney house opened, and Fiona came out, her reddish hair neatly braided. She saw Evie at her window and waved, smiling. Evie waved back, wondering if Fiona's brothers had said anything about what had happened. If they had, Evie would have to tell Fiona the truth or she would be scared, too.

Fiona believed in all sorts of haints and fairies and ghosts. A lot of people did, Evie knew. Not her Pa. And he lectured her every time she brought up Bloody Bones or Rawhead, or Jinns or Juok, or any of the others people had taught her about.

"Evie?"

"Coming!"

Evie took one last look across the street. Fiona was nearly to the end of the block. She was clever at figuring and writing and reading. Her parents didn't make her go to school. In fact, her mother wanted her to quit to help more at home with the laundry and cooking. But Fiona wanted to go, and for now, at least, her father was letting her.

Evie turned from her window, wondering if Mama would like it here. One thing she would like for sure was the Wheeler Wilson sewing machine Pa had bought for her. It was standing in the corner of her room, covered with an old blanket because her father wanted it to be a surprise. Not today, but later on. He said there was going to be enough joy in this day.

Evie lifted the blanket and touched the domed top of the fine-grained oak cover. The back of the cabinet was pretty well ruined where the crate had been dropped. But the front was perfect, and the machine worked silk smooth. Evie had tried it out, without thread in the needle. The treadle wheel spun so easily that the needle flashed up and down in a blur. Evie knew her mother would be thrilled beyond words to own such a machine.

Pa had been down on the levee to deliver work to the captain of the *Hiawatha*. They had been unloading damaged freight they'd bought at auction in Memphis. The dock man had dropped the sewing machine crate—again. It already had broken planks across the back.

Furious, the captain had sworn at the man, sure the machine would be ruined. Pa had offered him three dollars for the broken crate and whatever remained of the machine inside it. The captain had taken the money. Three dollars for a sewing machine! New ones cost seventy-five dollars or even more!

Evie lowered the blanket. Pa would give Mama the machine when she had her first bad dose of feeling homesick for her old farm and Kizzy and Sam and the rest. A real, foot-treadle sewing machine would raise Mama up out of any kind of sad time, Evie was pretty sure. She had wanted a sewing machine forever. Marse James was just too cheap.

"Evie?"

"Right now, Pa," she called back, pulling her dress straight.

"Good morning at last," Pa said as she came out. He already had a fire in the little hearth. On one side, Evie saw the spider skillet nestled into the raked-up mound of last night's coals.

"You hungry?"

Evie looked at him. "I just want the whole day to be over. I want Mama here and supper to be cooking, just us three."

"Soon enough," her father said quietly. "You don't want to miss the fun of the day, though, do you? We'll get to see Marse James pretend to be glad when he's counting out the money. And Mistress Florence will have to put on some fancy dress for us. She doesn't have near enough to do out there on that farm. I think if she had her way, she'd be on that omnibus every morning and not go back until the theaters and shops were all closed down."

"Mama says Mistress Florence hates the country," Evie said, shaking her head. "How can anyone hate a nice farm like that?"

Her father licked his forefinger, then touched the skillet lightly. It hissed. "People are foolish," he said. "They want what they can't have and don't want what they do have. White, black, brown, and yellow, and probably red, though I never knew any Indians to talk to. Nobody ever seems satisfied with what he's got."

"White people have whatever they want, though, Pa."

He shook his head. "No, they don't. It just seems that way. They have more than we do, sure enough. And that's wrong, no matter what they preach in church. But someday there will be no more slavery."

Evie watched his face. She had heard him talk like this many times, and as always he had lowered his voice to a whisper. There was no sense in calling trouble to the front door.

"Evie?"

She focused on his face. He was grinning. "You going to cook us some corn cakes? I'll go get Lucky and Ginger harnessed and bring them around to the front. You best get the eggs before we go—just so the Maloney boys don't."

Evie stared. "Have they been stealing eggs?"

"One or two a day, I think. Haven't you noticed we've been short?"

Evie ducked her head. She hadn't told him why the speckled hen wasn't laying. She busied herself pulling the cornmeal sack from the shelf. As she reached for the batter bowl she risked a glance at him. He was bent over, reaching beneath his cot for his boots.

Watching him sidelong, Evie saw him wipe dust from the leather before he sat on the edge of his cot to pull them on. He was proud of his boots. He switched feet every day to keep them wearing evenly. Once a year he had the soles replaced—and if he couldn't, he wore them with holes. He said bare feet on a grown man were the mark of a field slave.

Evie got down the batter bowl, then set it on the table her father had made the week they had moved in. He had used boards from a broken-down stall in the stable, recutting two of them to straighten tiny curves so they'd fit together smoothly. They had taken turns rubbing the planks with river sand until they were smooth and clean.

Evie hurried along, feeling fluttery as she got down the meal scoop and opened the cotton calico cornmeal sack. The fire, even though it was small, was heating up the kitchen enough to make a sheen of sweat on her brow.

Evie missed the old place most in the summer. Marse William's farm had four springs and a pond. Marse William said no one was supposed to swim on workdays, but everyone did and he pretended not to notice. His wife even looked the other way when the days got so hot the shade wasn't much better than the sun. Evie imagined how it had been, running with Kip and Cyprus and Harold and the others, their shirttails flapping in the wind, jumping out from the bank, the delicious cool water closing over her sweaty head.

Evie shook her head. Maybe someday they could have a farm of their own—with a creek and a swimming hole they could use any time they wanted with no one to say different.

Sighing, she used the hearth rake to stir the new fire, then added a piece of wood. She put an inch of water in the stew pot and pushed it as close to the little morning fire as she could. Then she turned back to the batter bowl.

"Hurry on, now," Pa said from the door.

Evie looked up and nodded. "Mama is going to be so happy," she said, and watched his face light with joy.

"I have waited my whole life for this day, Evie. Me, my wife, and my daughter . . . free." He whispered the last word, and Evie felt chill bumps on the back of her neck. It was too good to be true. Too wonderful to believe. Pa smiled and went out, closing the door solidly behind himself.

Measuring with a cup-shaped gourd, Evie dipped cool water from the well bucket into the bowl, then half as much cornmeal as the water. She beat the mixture until the pea-sized lumps had smoothed out, then added another cup of water and beat it again. The saleratus can was nearly empty, she realized as she opened it. She'd have to tell Pa or they'd be eating flat bread and heavy mush before long.

Evie smiled suddenly, realizing that Mama would tell him such things from now on. This would be Mama's kitchen, and she would run it as well as she had run Marse James's. Humming, Evie sprinkled a scant spoonful of sugar across the top of the batter and beat it in. Then she unwrapped the quarter side of bacon they'd been eating for a week. The smell was getting stronger. They'd best finish it in the next day or two.

Evie cut off a fat chunk of the bacon, then cut that into strips. She saw one skipper in the meat, wriggling to get away. She crushed it with the knife tip and cut that strip narrower, looking for more. She couldn't find any.

Evie laid the bacon strips in the hot skillet and listened to the instant hissing of the fat against the heated iron. She beat her batter a little longer, adding a pinch of salt and a smaller, extra pinch of sugar. Pa insisted on the sugar. When he was a boy, he never saw sugar—his master didn't believe in sugar for his slaves, only cornmeal and fatback, then a little flour and clabber on Sundays for biscuits.

"Evie?"

The whisper startled Evie. She dropped the spoon. It tilted off the edge of the bowl and clattered on the floor.

"Evie!"

Evie spun in a circle so she could see out the little window above her father's cot. There was no glass in it. He tacked up cheesecloth to keep the mosquitoes out. A silhouette was visible in the window frame, and Evie recognized Fiona.

"I saw you go off to school," Evie said as she crossed the room. "Why didn't you just come to the front door?"

Fiona glanced behind herself. "I didn't want Liam to see me. Or anyone else."

Evie pulled in a quick breath. "This morning I—"

"Don't tell me now," Fiona interrupted. "If I'm tardy Sister Charity will make me stand in the corner for an hour. Just look out for Liam and Sean. They're mad as wet hens about something. Tell your pa."

Evie shook her head, then realized Fiona

couldn't see. "I don't want to tell him."

"Then just you be on watch. I'm so sorry. . . ."

"It's not your fault," Evie said quickly.

"Today's when you go get your mama, isn't it?" Fiona asked.

"Yes." Evie heard Pa whistling and knew that Fiona had, too, because she looked toward the stable.

"Just watch out for the boys. I hope your mama is happy when she gets here."

"Thank you, Fiona," Evie said quietly, but Fiona was rustling her way back through the lilac bushes and probably couldn't hear.

CHAPTER FOUR

By the time her father walked back through the front door, Evie had four little corn cakes popping and bubbling in the skillet. She scooped them out with the slotted spoon so most of the grease stayed in the pan, then ladled in more batter. The edges frilled up in the hot grease, and the smell of hot corn filled the kitchen.

They sat at the plank table on overturned crates they had found down by the levee. There were three crates. They had found the first two side by side, whole and sound, only a little muddy. Pa had refused to give up after the first two. They had walked in circles for nearly an hour before the third whole crate turned up. They called it Mama's chair. Pa had sand-scoured it, and they kept it clean and set it at the table as though she was already there to use it.

They ate off two chipped plates Miss Ellia had given Evie the first week she had cleaned her house.

There were two more of the same set up on the shelf, without chips. Evie wanted to save them from everyday wear since they were still perfect. But that would soon be Mama's decision, too, Evie thought, standing to turn the last two corn cakes over in the grease.

"You are a fine cook," Pa said as she returned to the table, toeing her crate back so she could sit again. His face was lit with love for her, and Evie felt herself blushing.

"Your mama will be proud of how you've done here." He gestured at the tins and boxes on the shelves, neat and clean, the hearth stacked with kindling, the full wood box. The walls were freshly washed, and the cloudy glass of the old window was spotless. They had been getting ready for Mama for a long time now.

"Miss Ellia says I am smart."

Pa chewed, looking at her. "She is right about that."

Evie glanced up at the ceiling, then back at him. This was the wrong day to bring it up, she knew it. But she couldn't help it.

"What?" her father said. "What are you thinking about so hard?"

Evie bit at her lip. "You'll just say no."

"Maybe not." He lifted his fork but didn't eat, keeping his eyes on hers. "What, Evie?"

"Miss Ellia thinks I should go to Meachum's

floating school. She says there isn't a thing the law in Missouri can do about it. She said he takes a boat full of children out there every day of the world."

Pa didn't say anything for a moment. Then he cleared his throat. "Miss Ellia is white, Evie. She's a good woman, but she doesn't understand. Meachum's found a way to beat the law for now. But come the day they can burn that steamer he has anchored out there, they will. I don't want you caught up in something like that."

Evie squirmed on her crate, knowing he was probably right, but wishing she could go to a real school. "Fiona says the Sisters are—"

"It's the same," her father interrupted. "Can't you see that? They are good folks trying to do the right thing. But when trouble comes it'll skip their door and knock on ours. That's enough talk about school. Read the newspaper from the fish wrappers. Write every day in that accounting book like you promised Marse William and be glad you got as much learning as you got." He lifted a hand to prevent any response she had. "And you make sure you keep that book of Marse William's well hid. Don't ever take it out of this house, not even for a second."

"I won't, Pa," Evie promised. His face had gone stern, and she was sorry she had brought up school at all. She had known what his answer would be anyway. And he hadn't said it, but the truth was they needed her to work. Her wages helped.

"Are you about finished?"

Evie looked up at her father. "Almost. Just let me clean up so when we come back it looks nice for Mama."

Her father nodded. "I'll go chop wood so that's done, too. What else? Maybe we should draw water and get it in?"

"Sure, Pa," Evie agreed.

He carried his plate to the sideboard and grinned at her. "As long as we don't get there before Marse James has had his coffee and pipe, we won't be too early."

Evie nodded. Marse James was uncordial before his morning coffee—and his pipe was as important to him as just about anything. Pa picked up the ax from behind the door and slung it up onto his shoulder. Evie soon heard the hollow crack of the ax biting into firewood. After the first few cracks there was the musical clatter of the splits falling into a pile around the tree stump they used as a chopping block.

Evie found herself glancing out the window every few seconds as she poured the steaming wash water from the stew pot into the big tin-plated tub they used as both bath and washbasin.

Evie tried to make short work of their plates and spoons, then cleaned out the batter bowl. The lye soap stung her hands, and she noticed a ragged little cut on her thumb for the first time. Probably from climbing the tree so fast.

As she carried the wash water out onto the porch and across the yard, Evie glanced across Warren Street. The Maloneys would be embarrassed, trying to forget how scared they had been.

"'Bout done?" Pa called from the chopping block.

Startled out of her thoughts, Evie turned quickly. "Just have to dump the wash water and dry the tin."

There was a sheen of sweat on his forehead. The early sun was just now slanting through the tops of the cottonwoods.

Evie lugged the basin across the yard and swung it hard, turning in a circle so that the water would arc in a sheet away from her without spattering her dress. Mama always noticed new stains or tears in her clothes. Evie set the tub down for a second and searched the front of her dress, looking for snagged places from the tree. She arched around, trying to see over her own shoulder. Her father's chuckle made her turn to face him.

"Looking for something your mama will notice?" he asked.

She smiled.

"I think she'll be busy enough today without that, Evie."

Evie grabbed the tub. The steady hollow whacking of the ax began again as her father went back to work. She started for the house and was almost to the porch when Lucky whickered. Evie set the tub down once more and ran to pat both mares. "I'm sorry those boys scared you this morning," she told them, smoothing their foretops back away from their deep brown eyes. "I will see it doesn't happen again if I can." Lucky nickered softly once more as if to answer.

Evie went in the house, glancing around as she walked through, imagining what her mother would think when she first saw it. Mama had lived most of her life in Marse James's attic—in his fine house. This wasn't grand, that was sure. Evie hoped she would like it. It was a lot better than most slave cabins and it was *theirs*.

Back in the kitchen, Evie put things to rights, wiping the table clean, straightening their crates just so. She nudged the little jars of feverfew and sassafras bark into a straighter line on the shelf and brushed the ashes off the hearth into the fire. She carried in a fresh bucket of water and set it on the sideboard. Then she picked up the basin again.

The coarse, hemp feed sack Evie used to dry it

was still a little damp from the night before. She would have to get it out into the sun or it would mildew. Once hemp mildewed, it was impossible to get the sour smell out. Evie went out just as her father was coming up the porch steps. She held up the damp cloth. "It needs sun. And I want to wash my face, then I'm ready."

Pa smiled. "Good, Evie. Then we'll go." He went in.

Evie hung the cloth over the porch rail and walked across the yard to the well pump. She peered down the shaft. The prime was still high enough. She worked the handle three or four times, then bent to splash her face and neck. She stood on the rocks Pa had set into the ground to keep down the mud. She rubbed at her cheeks, then pumped the handle up and down three more times. She caught a double handful of the gush and splashed her face again.

Evie straightened, lifting her hem to pat her face dry. She was about to start back to the house when she noticed a quick movement across the street. Without seeming to watch, Evie stood still beside the pump, pretending to squint up at the sky, as if she were just guessing what the weather was going to be like.

There. Out of the corner of her eye she saw something move again. It wasn't straight across the street in the Maloneys' little dirt yard, but farther west, in front of the next house, where the Jenkinses lived. She almost never saw the elderly couple, not even out on their porch. A younger woman came once or twice a week—their daughter, Pa said.

Evie glanced back past the wagon at the door. Pa had closed it behind himself. She yawned and pretended to turn eastward, looking down Warren Street toward the river. The movement came once more, and this time Evie was sure it was someone watching her. One of the Maloneys? It had to be. They would probably do something once she and Pa were gone. Evie felt an uneasiness tighten her stomach. What would they do? Kill all the poor hens? Steal something? Evie thought about the boys going through the house, laughing at the chipped plates and the crates for chairs. They were just as poor, but she knew they looked down on her and her father anyway.

Evie could hear her father whistling inside. She squared her shoulders. The Maloneys had been angry with her before and they had never done more than play some trick. If she told her father now, it'd shadow his whole day—a day that should shine for him always. And for Mama. She looked up the street, narrowing her eyes to stare straight at the tree that hid her watcher. "Don't you dare do anything to tarnish this day for us," she whispered.

"Evie?"

"I'm ready, Pa," she answered, turning. She climbed up into the wagon, settling on the hard oak plank next to her father as he gathered up the reins and clicked his tongue at Lucky and Ginger. He backed them up far enough to make the turn out the narrow drive onto Warren Street. Evie stared hard at the tree as they passed, but she couldn't see anyone there now. She glanced back twice, hoping to catch Liam or Sean out of hiding, but the street was empty.

Lucky and Ginger pulled the wagon out of the dusty drive, the oaken planks of the bed creaking as the wheels rose, then dropped into the deep ruts left from the last hard rain. Evie gripped the edge of the driver's bench to keep from being thrown off the seat.

"You be good today," Pa said.

"I will," Evie promised.

"We don't need extra trouble."

"I know, Pa."

He reached out to pat her hand, and she knew he didn't mean to scold her. He was just nervous. So was she.

"Everything starts over today," Pa said softly.

CHAPTER FIVE

Once the wagon was straightened around and going alongside the worst of the ruts, Pa flicked the reins over the mares' rumps. Ginger switched her tail and put her ears back, shuffling into a reluctant trot. Lucky, as always, was willing and good-natured. She leaned into her collar and pulled Ginger along a little faster. The difference between the two mares was so obvious it was comical.

Evie watched her father shake his head, laughing. "Ginger, don't drag your old self along too slow today. Didn't I tell you where we are going?"

Evie smiled. "She doesn't care, Pa."

He grinned and sat up tall on the driver's bench. His broad back and shoulders were muscled from his work, and he looked proud and strong sitting so straight. "This errand is so important, even ignorant animals need to know about it," he teased. Then he leaned forward. "We are going to get my wife, you fool horse, and I don't want to hear no more never-mind about it!" He made his voice high and squeaky, like an old woman shooing children away from whatever they were supposed to stay out of.

Evie laughed again, her uneasiness beginning to dissolve in the glow of early sunlight and her father's joyous mood. The wagon bumped over a curving rut where Warren crossed Broadway. A man, driving a carriage with matched bays, whipped up his team, and Pa reined in to let them pass. There was a little Negro boy clinging to the footman's perch on the back of the carriage. Pa grinned at him and he smiled back, but didn't loosen his grip on the leather hand loop to wave. Evie saw two young women inside the carriage as it went by.

One had auburn hair piled in ringlets into a great mound atop her head. As the carriage passed, she turned slowly to look out the window, keeping her chin level. It reminded Evie of the way Mama moved when she had a laundry basket balanced on her head. Evie wished she could see their dresses. They were probably fancy, with stiff crinoline petticoats, or even the new light wooden hoops Mama had told her about.

Once the white folks' carriage had gone by, Pa flicked the reins again, and Ginger switched her tail. Lucky tossed her head, impatient for Ginger's morning moodiness to pass.

"Looks like she is not going to listen to you today, no matter what you tell her."

Pa laughed. "Looks like it." Then he dropped his voice and leaned closer so that he could speak very quietly. "Evie? There was an advertisement in the *Missouri Republican* yesterday, telling about some trees Alexander and Lansing shipped in from China. All the way from China. Imagine that."

Evie whistled and nodded. Pa always read the newspapers that were used to wrap fish or vegetables down at Center Market—but he would not dare buy one. Any Negro walking around with a book or a newspaper was asking to be jailed and sold South. Evie wrinkled her forehead, trying to remember if anyone had ever told her where China was. Her mother had used silk from China to make special dresses for Mistress Florence. "Is China that far off? Farther than New Orleans?"

Pa nodded. "It's farther than almost anywhere, Marse William told me once. He said they have cities there a thousand years old, some of them even more."

Evie could only stare at him. He laughed at her expression and reached out to teasingly push her chin up to close her mouth. "So, do you think we ought to go buy your mama a tree from China? You know how she loves to plant and tend things."

Evie lifted her eyebrows. "You have any money?"

He nodded. "A little above the rent this month. Not much." He lowered his voice again. "The advertisement didn't say how much the trees would cost."

A steamboat blew its whistle, and Evie looked down toward the river. It was the *A. G. Mason,* a big rear-wheeler, a mail packet on its way South. "It's on Locust between Second and Third, the ad said." Pa glanced around. There were people standing on the corner of Broadway and Market as they made the turn. A tall white man was nailing a poster to the corner post. Evie glanced at it, only able to make out one word at the top, written in big, fancy script: CIRCUS.

"I saw that in the paper, too," her father said quietly. "They have acrobats, a clown, and elocutionists. Animals, too, maybe lions—or so Clem down at the market said. And there was something about a female rider. It didn't say if they had seats for colored. Usually do." He looked at her sidelong. "Couldn't do that and get the tree, too."

Evie shrugged, thinking. "Mama would like the tree best," she said finally.

Her father sighed. "Probably. It'd be something that'd last. You know how she is about that."

Evie nodded. Mama always preferred something solid and useful to something that was fun, then gone.

Pa shrugged. "We'll see another circus someday."

"You never saw one, either, Pa?"

He shook his head. "But now we can do more what we want. We'll get to a circus."

Evie smiled at him, then loud voices made her turn and look down Madison Street, toward the river. A half block or so down toward the dry docks, three white men were shouting at each other at the top of their lungs in the middle of the street. Two or three wagons had stopped, unable to get past.

One man stepped back, nearly losing his balance. Evie stared. The men weren't shouting at each other. There was a boy, a little boy. He was holding a hoop in one hand, a push stick in the other. There was something about the way he stood, his uneven haircut.

"Pa," Evie said. "That's Terrence Maloney." She pointed. Something was shining on the ground around Terrence's feet. Cans? There were papers, too, folded flat like wrapped butter or meat. Someone's groceries?

Pa turned to squint into the early sun. "You sure? Where are all his brothers?"

"I don't know, but they—"

Terrence's terrified shout stopped her midsentence. One of the men had raised his fist. Evie gasped as the man struck Terrence on the side of his head. Terrence sprawled onto the street, wailing. One of the men laughed.

"Lord, but I hate to see men getting drunk like that," Evie heard her father mutter. "I can't walk up and tell them to stop, you know that."

Evie nodded, staring helplessly. Then, a sudden jolt of the wagon startled her. Her father was turning the mares down Madison. She stared at the men. Sometimes Mr. Maloney drank until he was staggering. It made Fiona ashamed, Evie could tell, so she never talked about it. Liam and the boys didn't seem to care much. Their father usually just shouted for a while, at nothing, then lay down and went to sleep like a child, curled up in their yard or on their porch swing.

"What do you think happened?" Pa asked in a low voice as they got closer.

Evie shrugged. "He was probably rolling that hoop instead of looking where he was going."

Terrence's head was lowered, but she could see that his cheek was cut. Evie looked past him to the wagons beyond. There were four now, all waiting to pass. A sharp cry brought her eyes back. The man had slapped Terrence again.

"Oh, my Lord," Pa breathed.

Evie stared at her father. He met her eyes. "If I go interfere with a white man, I'll end up in front of a judge, or worse."

Terrence yelled again, and Evie winced without looking. Pa was scowling, fierce. "Evie, run up and tell Terrence his mama says he has to come home with us, right now. Say it as loud as you can and make sure everyone hears you. Don't touch the man, or Terrence. And for God's sake don't let anyone get close enough to reach you. Anything happens, you run straight back to me."

Evie nodded, sliding down from the driver's bench. The sharp gravel of the street hurt her feet as she ran toward Terrence. The drunken man still stood over him.

"Your mama says you have to come on home with us now!" Evie yelled it over the thudding of her heart. She was breathing hard, even though she hadn't run very far. Startled, the man turned. Evie saw groceries scattered around him, a plucked chicken lying in the gritty street dust.

"Your mama wants you to come with us right now!" Evie shouted again. Terrence stood, blinking at her without moving. Evie waited, willing him to react, wondering what she could do if he didn't. People were coming out of the shops and houses to see what the yelling was about.

"Hey!" The shout came from the wagoner stopped on the other side of the men. "Don't let him go on with this, son. Run along home with your colored gal." The wagoner had a booming voice, and the drunken man looked up, frowning, realizing for the first time that he had an audience. "It ain't all the boy's fault. You wasn't watching where you was going, either!" There were cries of assent from both sides of the street.

"Come on," Evie hissed at Terrence. "Come with me now."

The man suddenly stepped back, bending over to pick up his groceries, moving in clumsy, embarrassed circles. Terrence touched a short, deep cut over his right eyebrow. There were welts rising along his cheek and neck. He tucked his stick and hoop under one arm and stooped to pick up the chicken, trying to wipe the road sand off it with his sleeve. The man snatched it from him and shoved it into his straw bag. Then he walked off, his friends trailing behind him.

The wagoner in the first wagon cheered, and other raucous voices joined in. Blood was trickling down Terrence's face from the cut. "Pa's over there," she said, gesturing. Looking dazed, he followed her and scrambled up into the back of the wagon when she gave him a boost.

Pa clucked at the mares and got them moving again. "Here, son, take this." He turned to hold out a clean kerchief.

Terrence sat down with a lurch as the wagon

started to roll forward. He set down his hoop and stick and reached for the handkerchief. "Thank you."

"You are very welcome," Pa said. "We'll get you home where your mama can tend your hurts."

Evie hopped into the back of the wagon and sat cross-legged, as far away from Terrence Maloney as she could get. Pa turned the wagon around and Ginger whickered, happy to be headed back to her stall.

"Thank you," Terrence said again, dabbing at his face with Pa's kerchief.

"Pa told me to," Evie said, looking past him at the people on the sidewalk. Pa made such a sharp turn back onto Broadway that Evie had to grab the sideboard to keep from tipping over. She tried not to look at Terrence's poor, bruised face. She had wanted to help him. But now, with him sitting this close, all she could think about was all the mornings of name-calling and thrown rocks and her speckled hen, tied onto that high limb, terrified and trembling.

Once they were back on Warren Street, Pa turned again to look at Terrence. "You want help getting in?"

Terrence shook his head. "My ma will be there."

Pa pulled the mares to a stop. Without another word Terrence let go of the bloody handkerchief and slid to the rear of the wagon. He got down, clutching his stick and hoop, and walked across the barren little yard toward the back door.

Pa swung the mares around once more, and Ginger shook her head in disappointment as they started off a second time. Back on Broadway, Evie watched the cross streets go by, reading the signs on the corner posts: Benton, Monroe, Madison, Chambers. Broadway angled to stay parallel with the river, and the scattered line of wagons rounded the curve.

A wagon loaded with dried moss rumbled up Webster Street, pulling in front of them. Pa slowed to give the driver room. Evie stared at the dull green mound in the back of the wagon. It shivered and shifted with every bump of the wagon.

"That's what I need for the new mattress," Pa said, pointing.

Evie nodded. "Miss Ellia has a niece getting married in her parlor. She'll need extra cleaning, laundry, extra serving. I'll have more pay than usual."

"I'd like this first day or two to be perfect for your mama," Evie heard her father say softly, talking to himself.

Evie reached out to touch his forearm lightly. He had wanted to have the bed finished, the house all fixed up. He had talked about real curtains for the windows and a new oil cloth for the floor, too, but they hadn't been able to manage that much.

For a few minutes they rode in silence. Evie kept glancing at her father. A thoughtful expression had come over his face and it dulled the joy that had been there all morning. She wondered what he was thinking, but she knew better than to ask. When he got quiet like this, it was because he wanted to mull something over by himself.

Evie turned and faced the river. She could see a steamboat making its way north against the swirling flood of brown water. She could see the far side of the river this morning. Sometimes, if it was misty, she couldn't.

They passed Brooklyn Street, then Mound. Businesses were bustling. Wagons crisscrossed the roadway, drivers shouting at each other for more room. Half the importers' and agents' offices had merchandise stacked in the street, making it narrower.

They passed Howard Street, then Mulanphy. Evie looked down each one as they went by. All the streets below the upper ferry ended in a blunt drop-off, a steep, muddy incline down to the river, where the dry docks began. Along both sides of Broadway people were appearing now, walking with their collars turned up against the morning coolness as they made their way to work.

"Good morning, Mr. Peach, Evie!"

Evie turned to see Mr. Garner, a friend of Willis's and her father's. His starched jacket stood out against the drab coats and shirts of the men around him. Not all barbers were as crisp and clean as Mr. Garner, but it was his trademark. His shop was on Fourth Street, down by Wood's Theater. He had light skin—his family had been in St. Louis, free, for a hundred years. His shop mostly catered to the carriage trade. Evie smiled at him and waved shyly as they went past. She liked Mr. Garner. He was handsome—always so polite and fancy in his manners. He was more a gentleman than Marse James would ever be.

"Look."

Evie followed her father's gesture. Ahead of the moss wagon, a fine carriage was rounding the corner from Biddle Street onto Broadway, coming down the hill. This time the team was well bred: matched sorrels with flashing blazes and stockings. "Now, there's another smart turnout. Look at the nickel plate on the harness." Evie nodded without really looking. Pa never got tired of looking at well-made carriages and harness and highbred horses.

As Pa guided the mares through the gentle curve that marked Broadway's change into Third Street, the traffic thickened. Slowing to allow the other wagons and carts and carriages to get across or make turns, they passed through the big intersection where Cass Street met Second on the west side, and Columbia joined Second Street on the east. Evie looked down Columbia to the dry docks. There were five or six steamers lined up. She could see workmen pointing and talking.

"A lot of folks up and going early this morning," Evie's father said, reining in as a boy darted in front of the mares. He carried a big, covered delivery basket. Evie stared at it. It was probably full of fresh bread or pastries. Her mouth watered.

The next double intersection was at O'Fallon Street. The sharp smell of burnt sugar from the Belcher Sugar Refinery drifted all the way up from the river. There were men and women walking toward the big six-story building, even this early. Belcher's had a lot of jobs. When she was old enough, Fiona said she thought she might try to work there. Pa said Belcher paid a fair wage, to white or black, man or woman.

Storekeepers were unrolling their awnings now. Evie saw people who had driven in early and waited for stores to open climbing down off their wagon seats. There were still quite a few covered wagons in town. Evie had seen them come every spring of her whole life—come and go. By June there would be many fewer wagons with their plodding oxen to clog up the streets. People left in early summer to make the trek Westward—or they waited until the next year.

"Maybe we should go West," Pa said, like he always did when they saw a bunch of the wagons with their stiff, sturdy Osnaberg covers. Evie didn't answer him. She knew in a minute or so he would answer himself. "Your mama would never go," he said.

"Let her get used to one thing at a time," Evie said, and Pa laughed.

"For a girl barely out of shirttail shifts, you sound pretty wise," he said. Evie smiled at him.

Locust Street was coming up. Pa worked the mares in a line that angled them toward the center of the street. They went up over three sets of ruts, the wheels lurching in and out. Evie hung on, waiting for her father to rein Ginger and Lucky to a stop. When he did, she loosened her grip and stared at the stream of wagons and people coming toward them. Maybe there would be a Negro driver who would let them turn before too long. Evie heard her father start to hum.

She tried to imitate him, staring off as though the people going by were no concern of hers. He kept humming as two or three freight wagons passed. One driver was swearing at his team in a language Evie had never heard before. He had blue eyes and dark curling hair. Evie tried to watch without staring. He looked Irish, but all the Irish spoke English—in their own odd way. She kept an eye on him as he went by, turning down Locust Street. He called out to a friend, and Evie heard the man answer in the same strange words. Then she couldn't hear or see either of them anymore.

"Oh, Lord. Good thing your mama isn't with us," Evie heard her father say.

Evie turned to look and caught her breath.

CHAPTER SIX

Of course, Evie thought. They were less than three blocks away from Lynch's. And Tuesday was often a sale day there. So they were bringing slaves in now. Evie swallowed, trying to look away, but she couldn't. She could feel her own pulse like a rabbit's, quick and helpless as she watched two big men marching a group of Negroes along Third Street.

"On their way down to Lynch's," Pa said in a flat tone of voice.

Evie nodded. One of the women looked pregnant. She was stumbling along, her cheeks wet with tears. There were two old men and two older women—and three boys who wore shirttails with nothing on underneath. They were thirteen or fourteen, at least. Evie cringed. She had worn a shirttail shift like that, but not after she was eight. Marse William had all his slaves dress decent once they grew up.

"They're plantation slaves," Pa said quietly. "Or runaways, maybe."

The little group made their way through a tangle of crates and boxes stacked in front of a grocery store. Some of the crates were marked SUGAR. Others said COFFEE. Evie shook her head. Those were two things that slaves nearly never got and here they had to wade through the crates, quick-stepping, the two big men herding them along.

"Oh, Lord," Pa breathed.

The pregnant woman was crying so hard, she was awkward getting through the crates. She made one false step as Evie watched, then another. Then, she slipped off the rough curb and fell. One of the older men helped her back onto her feet. The slave drivers gripped her shoulder, speaking urgently into her face.

"She's pregnant," Evie said, unable to think of anything else to say. Her hands were sweating, and her stomach was sick. Pa didn't answer.

They watched as the two big men escorted the group across the street. Both the boys were wide-eyed, nearly falling over their own feet. On the far side, they threaded a path through bales of cloth.

"They've never been in a town before, Pa," Evie whispered.

"And may never be again," her father

answered. "They'll never see anything but cotton and red dirt and killing work again."

"You going to turn or sit there all damn day?"

Evie twisted around. A burly white man driving a delivery cart had come up behind them.

"Sorry, Marse," Evie's father called out, ducking his head as he spoke, shaking the reins. Ginger switched and shambled, and Evie saw her father pull the whip out of its boot and lash her once, hard. She leaned into the harness, and the wagon rolled forward.

They creaked and lurched across the ruts, the driver behind them still cursing quietly as he whipped up his mules to trot past, getting onto Locust Street first. He kept his team going, yelling at a dark-suited man lugging two sample cases across the street. The sales agent didn't look at the driver, just stepped up onto the sidewalk and disappeared into a shop beneath a red awning.

"It's a warehouse," Pa said, bending to talk into Evie's ear. "Company name of Alexander and Lansing."

Evie nodded and let her eyes slide across the street, searching the cluttered storefronts. She spotted a placard in front of one door. She couldn't read it this far away, but it had a drawing of a tree on the top. "It's on the other side, I think," she said to her father. "Up almost a block." She made out the names emblazoned on the awning. ALEXANDER & LANSING. She gestured broadly. "The blue awning. "

"Whoa!" The driver of the wagon in front of them shouted. Evie's father pulled on the reins, and the mares stopped. Evie watched the driver vault down. Once he had his team secured to the hitching rail, he came around to the back of the wagon and flung open the freight doors. There were long rolls of carpet inside—or maybe oilcloth or linoleum, Evie couldn't tell. He glanced up at her and her father, then away, his face unreadable, as if he hadn't seen them stuck behind his wagon.

Evie's father leaned out, trying to see past. "He's not going to move even a little for us. Go take a look."

Evie waited for a man with a crate of apples to pass her side of the wagon. Then she scrambled down. Once she was on the sidewalk, she was careful not to brush against anyone. A woman wearing heavy silk and heavier perfume scowled and lifted her wide skirts as Evie passed. Peering through the crowds, Evie spotted an opening at one of the hitching rails farther down.

Evie climbed up onto the seat as her father clucked at the mares, easing them sideways more than forward, so that the wagon wheels had turned a little before they started on around the freight wagon.

The instant they began to move, the passing drivers cursed and whipped up their teams rather than give way. A Negro man driving a span of eight mules hitched to a wagon with fancy red lettering on the side slowed just enough to let them in. He lifted a hand in greeting, and Evie's father returned it. Evie read the lettering as they passed: HOOD AND LANGAN'S CITY BLACKSMITH SHOP.

"I buy my iron stock off them sometimes," Pa said as they pulled out into the line of wagons. "His name is Otis. He hates me 'cause I'm free. But he's such a good Christian, he can't let it show. So he is decent and friendly to me, even though I can see the hate in his eyes. I don't blame him a whit. He near kills himself on that forge for his master. If I had money like Meachum, I'd buy that one out. Otis would pay me back quick to get himself free."

"Meachum's helped a lot of folks get free, Miss Ellia says," Evie said cautiously. She didn't want him to get started on the floating school again.

"That's a fact," Pa said mildly. "Lots of good folks trying to do the right thing. Including Miss Ellia. I know that."

Evie shot him a grateful smile. He frowned.

"There are just as many trying to keep their money in their pockets, too, Evie. Never mind that they are buying and selling souls—and they know it's damnable wrong." Evie glanced around. No one had heard. Mama was always afraid Pa's mouth would land him in trouble.

They were opposite the long wharf now. Steamboats were tied up in a slanting line along it, their lacy fretwork gleaming in the morning sun. Beneath and beyond them, the river ran dark and wide. The smell of wet sand filled Evie's nostrils.

Pa swung the team wide, making a long, slow turn that headed them back where they had come from, but on the right side of the street this time.

"There?"

Evie nodded. "The blue awning."

He angled the team toward the placard that stood on a wooden easel on the sidewalk. As they got closer, Evie could read it:

EVERGREENS—JUST ARRIVED, THE FINEST LOT OF
CHINESE ARBORVITAES (FINE, PYRAMIDAL FORM)
EVER SEEN IN ST. LOUIS. ALSO A FEW PLANTS OF THE
LINGSTRUM LINEUSES, A SPLENDID EVERGREEN TREE.
THE WHOLE TO BE SOLD ON REASONABLE TERMS,
CASH TERMS ONLY, AT THIS WAREHOUSE OF:
ALEXANDER & LANSING. AGENTS WELCOME.

Evie turned away. She saw a white man staring at her, and her heart froze. Her eyes slid away from his, and she climbed down from the wagon seat just as Pa did, afraid to risk even one more glance at the man. How could she have been so stupid? To just sit there reading in the middle of the street?

"Evie?"

She ducked under the mares' necks and caught up as her father stepped up onto the sidewalk. Through a doorway, Evie spotted a mass of bright green. As she watched, a Negro man raised a watering can, then lowered it, moving on a half step, then raising it again.

"Evie."

She felt her father's hand on her shoulder and looked up. He gestured with his chin. A white man and woman had come in behind them. Evie stepped aside.

"No, no, that's all right," the man said. "We'll take our turn." The woman nodded and smiled.

Evie looked down at the floor, unsure what to do. Her father squeezed her shoulder and nudged her forward. "I thank you kindly," he said in a low voice.

Evie didn't want to look at the smiling couple, so she moved a little closer to the open door to see the man with the watering can. He was moving slowly, deliberately, pouring water into boxes full of wood shavings. Hanging out of the boxes every which way were odd-shaped fans of flat, needley leaves.

The man at the front of the line was speaking to the agent in low, urgent tones. The agent was shaking his head, a look of concern on his face. Finally the agent looked up, as if noticing the little line of people for the first time.

"I'm sorry, sir," he said clearly, a little too loudly. "Cash terms are the rule here."

The man took a quick step back and tipped his hat. Then he turned and hurried out.

The next customer was an elderly white man with spectacles. He nodded at everything the agent said, as though he already knew all there was to know about the little trees that had been shipped halfway around the world. In less than a minute, he was pulling coins from his pocket and handing them to the agent.

"Pack up a dozen of the Platycladus orientalis," the sales agent called through the open door. The man watering the trees set down the can.

"That'll be thirty-six dollars, sir," the agent said.

Evie glanced at her father. Thirty-six dollars for a dozen plants? That meant they were three dollars apiece.

"Maybe we ought to do this later on," her father said casually, his hand back on her shoulder.

Evie nodded, and they excused themselves to the nice couple behind them and made their way back outside. Evie saw her father shake his head. "Well, that was a waste of time."

Evie pulled herself up and settled on the bench, pulling her dress close around her legs. "You had no way to know, Pa." Her eyes strayed to a wall of runaway notices on the building next door. The reward numbers jumped out at her. One had a hundred-dollar reward for a male Negro, thirty years old, trained as a blacksmith. Evie looked aside. Maybe the blacksmith had made it to Illinois on the other side of the river. She hoped so.

"We could have been halfway to Marse James's by now." Pa was gathering the reins. Evie glanced down the block toward Lynch's, wondering if the people they had seen were there now, scared about ending up South.

A familiar face in the crowd caught her eye and she blinked, waiting until people moved on so she could see more clearly. For a cold, sharp instant of time, Liam Maloney seemed to be looking back at her. Then he dodged sideways and disappeared into the crowd.

CHAPTER SEVEN

Evie twisted around on the bench so many times that her father finally set one hand on her neck and clamped her into stillness. "What, Evie? Is something wrong or do you just have ants in your drawers?" He smiled to let her know he was teasing.

Evie shook her head. "Nothing's wrong." She stared straight ahead, trying to calm herself down. She was not going to tell him that she had seen Liam. That would mean telling him the whole story about the stable—probably about the hen, too. And all of that would lead to admitting how often they were ugly to her. And that, Evie knew, could easily lead to Pa saying something to Mr. Maloney. Evie pressed her lips together, aware that her father was watching her sidelong out of the corner of his eye.

"You bothered about something?" her father asked after a minute or two. He was pulling the team toward the center of the street to skirt a mud hole in front of a tavern.

Evie shook her head. "No, Pa."

A few men leaned against the front wall of the saloon, their eyes dull and their shoulders rounded. There were torn broadsides from the election still up on the wall. Evie saw Howe's name in bold letters. She had been glad when it was over and Howe had won. He had been mayor once before, then quit, Pa said, then he had run again. The Irish tavern a block above their house had fights over politics—the shouting carried a long way in the still of night.

"Evie?" Pa pressed her. "Are you disappointed about the China trees?"

Evie shook her head and made herself smile so he would quit asking her. "Mama would like a peach tree better anyway, Pa. Or an apple."

He nodded, and Evie saw relief on his face. "You're right. We could get her an apple tree once she's settled. Plant it right in front there. Mr. Wilkins won't mind. He's a good landlord." Evie watched him, realizing *he* had been the disappointed one. "The China tree seemed like such a perfect present," he said without looking at her.

"I know she'd like an apple tree better, Pa. She'd rather make a pie any day than daydream about where some old tree came from."

Pa reached over and tugged one of her braids. "You are smart. Miss Ellia is right about that much."

Evie let him pull her braid once more, then swatted at his fingers. He laughed and took the reins in both hands again. "We'll drop down to Chestnut Street, then get turned around and go back west to Olive. It'll be easier. Even with the omnibuses, it won't be as crowded this time of day as that Third Street section." He jiggled the reins, and Ginger rippled her skin like she was shaking off a fly. "I told you this is a special day, you old lazy," Pa scolded her.

Evie sat back, thinking about Mama. This was a happy day, and it was silly to waste time thinking about Liam and his brothers. In fact, it was good that Liam wasn't at home. Without Liam to start the trouble, the Maloneys would be much less likely to do anything at all. Evie exhaled and felt her stomach knot loosen.

"I do hope that Marse James won't make us take all day at this. Your mama will be fit to strangle if he does." Pa pulled the outside rein and started Lucky and Ginger into a long, easy turn down Second Street. Once the wagon tongue was straight again, he shook the reins and clicked his tongue, then slapped Ginger lightly across the rump with the reins. She hunched up for a step or two, but broke into a jog. Lucky kept the pace, tossing her head. Pa glanced at Evie. "There'll be papers to read and sign, I know. You be careful."

Evie nodded. "And you, too."

A block or so ahead of them was City Hall and the new post office. City Hall had a dozen freight wagons clustered beside it. It always did, except on Sunday. Evie wasn't sure what all the workmen were doing, but it seemed to her like City Hall had had men working on it like a kicked anthill all of her life.

As they rolled past the courthouse, Evie saw a few men in the slave pen. There was an estate auction today. For the hundredth time she looked heavenward and thanked Marse William for setting her free with her father. He could have kept her for one of his daughters.

In their manumission papers, Marse William had written that he felt he owed Pa his freedom because during all the years Pa had been hired out, he'd had opportunities to run away, but never did. All Marse William had said about Evie was that she was at the beginning of her life and he hoped she made a good and pious woman of herself.

Evie looked sideways at her father. Marse James owed Mama every bit as much as Marse William had owed Pa. He hired her out nearly every winter, and he kept every dime of the money. She hadn't expected to keep her wages, of course, but he had expected her to do the hire-out work and keep sewing for his family, too. That left Mama no time at all of her own—not even Saturday afternoons, like most slaves—and Marse James knew she was trying to save up to buy herself out.

If it had been up to Marse James, Mama would have died a slave. But she wasn't going to. She had saved three hundred dollars. And Pa had saved four. But even the money might not have been enough if it hadn't been for Mistress Florence.

The rhythm of the mares' hooves picked up a little as Pa urged them into a jog past the courthouse. Workmen swinging sledges were breaking up a low brick wall on one side. They shouted back and forth over the din of their hammering. Evie watched a brick mason working. He troweled mortar up out of a wide bucket and spread it deftly onto the top layer of brick in three quick strokes. Then he picked up a brick from the pallet beside the wall and set it, tapping it into place with the handle of his trowel. His motions were as smooth as honey in hot weather.

"What are you so quiet about, Evie?" Pa asked, once they were past the pounding and shouting of the city hall work crews.

Evie smiled up at him. "I was thinking about how much we owe Mistress Florence."

Pa nodded. "Indeed we do. If it was just Marse James—"

"That's what I mean," Evie said. "But he'll keep his word, won't he?"

Pa nodded. "He will. He'll just make it hard on your mama. She is so devoted to Mistress Florence, it's going to be strange for her to leave, no matter how much she wants to."

"Mistress Florence is kind, but Mama loves us and—"

"Your mama loves that white woman and don't you ever forget it," Pa interrupted. "Mistress Florence saved your life."

Evie stared at him. "My life? When?"

"Before you was born. Your mama was having early pains—it got too hard on her to work in the fields. Marse James wasn't listening. So she snuck up to the back door next evening. Mistress Florence brought your mama up to the house and fed her up on good table food and cosseted her. So your mama carried you to birth when it had looked like she would lose you."

Evie stared out across Chestnut Street, her stomach tightening up again. But, she thought, surprised at her reaction, it was a good story. She liked Mistress Florence fine. It was a good thing to know about her, wasn't it? But Evie didn't feel right for some reason. She twisted one foot, grinding her callused sole against the rough plank of the footrest.

"Marse James is a cruel man, for all his honey-talk," Evie's father said. "Mistress Florence is more like folks ought to be. To your mama, that seems extra-special."

Evie nodded, suddenly understanding her uneasy feelings. Mistress Florence had only done what anyone *should* do.

"Look out, ahead! Make way!"

The shout came from behind them. Evie turned. Her father shot a glance over his shoulder, but at the same time he was already pulling at the outside rein, veering the mares toward the side of the street. Evie saw a team of four big shaggy-coated draft horses barreling toward them. The driver was standing, hauling back on the reins, shouting at the top of his lungs for people to get out of the way. As Evie watched, two old women barely managed to scuttle across the street to safety.

The driver's mop of blond hair was trailing behind him, and Evie could see fear in his face as they got closer. There were flour barrels in the wagon bed, stacked in tight. The hundred-weight barrels bounced like children's spinning tops as the wagon heaved and lurched, crossing a rut.

Evie's father managed to get the mares over far

enough that the terrified team thundered past, passing their wagon so close that Lucky squealed in terror. People took up the driver's cry as the horses galloped on. A carriage team a half block ahead of them broke into a gallop as the runaways swept past. Evie watched the Negro driver trying to control them. She heard a scream from inside the carriage as the horses lunged, jolting the passengers.

"Whoa!" Pa shouted at Lucky when she danced against the harness. Ginger was wide-eyed and shaking, but she stood still. The wagoner was managing to slow his horses as they disappeared from sight up Chestnut Street. Pa clucked at the mares to go on. Lucky started off, snorting and nervous, drawing Ginger along with her.

They turned onto Twelfth Street, just a block before Washington Square. The park was empty now, but there would be children there later, and older people strolling the paths. Pa threaded through the delivery wagons around Lucas Market. For a half block the crush was as bad as it had been on Third Street. Then Pa pulled Ginger and Lucky to the left onto Olive Street. Here, the wagon wheels grated on the macadamized roadway, crunching across the gravel that had been worked into the soil in layers to harden it. The wheels rolled so much easier that Lucky pricked her ears and rose from a jog into a smart trot without urging, forcing a less willing Ginger along.

Olive Street was wide and clean, sloping upward. There were a few mansions along it, and Evie loved to stare at the brickwork and the gardens, wondering what it would be like to live in such a place. She could see an omnibus. The top-heavy horse cars always looked to her like they were about to tip over. The driver was a big, fierce-looking man with brown hair and ruddy skin. Most of the drivers were Irish, Evie knew. Their boss was the king of all the fist-fighters up on Battle Row.

There were people crowding the sidewalks here, and Evie watched the dark-suited men in their little round hats walking briskly. On the corners they stopped and gauged the traffic before they wove their way across the street. One man was walking so fast that he had to hold his hat on with one hand. Evie saw him pull his watch from his waistcoat pocket with the other hand and look at the time, all without slowing his step.

"Evie," Pa said, barely moving his lips. He jutted his chin out. "Look there."

A mulatto woman dressed in a shining purple skirt—so wide that people had to stop and step aside to let her pass—was sweeping her way down the sidewalk. She had a fan in one hand and a parasol swung from her wrist. Two men had to step into the street to give her room. An older woman stopped to gape and frown openly as she passed.

The woman acted as though nothing were amiss, nothing untoward about the scuffle she was causing. As they passed her, Evie forced herself not to stare. But the instant they were by, she half turned on the seat, pretending to straighten her own faded dress. The woman walked with her head so high and her spine so straight, it looked almost silly. And her corseted waist was cinched in so tight, it was a wonder she could breathe.

"Quite a turnout," Pa said, his voice low.

Evie nodded. "I'm glad Mama doesn't like hoops."

"No woman who wears hoops and a corset that tight is good for anything *but* mincing along a sidewalk," Pa said scornfully.

Evie nodded. There was another omnibus a half block behind them. The team was trotting smartly along. When it caught them up, Evie watched it slide past, full of white people dressed up like Sunday.

There were more shops here, fewer warehouses. Ladies often came here for hats and millinery goods or fashions copied from French patterns. The macadamized street was a big attraction to women whose expensive hemlines brushed the ground with every step. Here, at least for a few blocks, there was no sea of mud to ruin clothing and shoes.

As they passed out of the city, Evie realized she could hear the sound of their own wheels again. In town the noise never stopped. Someday, she wanted to live on a farm again. She wanted her very own place. Pa said there was a law that said even white women didn't own anything as long as their husbands were alive. Maybe she could marry someone who had a farm. Or someone who wanted a farm and they could work toward it together the way Mama and Pa had worked for her freedom.

Evie saw the tollgate not too far ahead. Today Mama would ride back through that gate, and if the man got nosy and asked to see slave passes, they could tell him to look at Mama's sale papers and their license receipts and hush him up.

Evie smiled. If anyone asked them who their master was, they could all say they just plain didn't have one anymore. "What are you grinning for?" Pa asked. Evie explained. He laughed. "That's so," he said, clucking to the mares. "We don't any of us need a pass. That's so, isn't it?"

CHAPTER EIGHT

The tollgate man didn't ask anything. He just took their coins and let them through. Pa got the mares trotting along. Evie was jittering on the bench like skippers in hot skillet fat.

Marse James had a long drive lined with maple trees. It ran through a cornfield. The corn was up about a foot, the rows clean and free of weeds.

"Maybe best you wait with the wagon," Pa said as they passed the whitewashed stable.

"Pa—"

"It's best," he repeated.

Evie fell silent, glaring straight ahead. She did not want to sit in the wagon wondering what was going on. "Please, Pa."

He shook his head. "Marse James will keep his word, but we just don't know what else might happen. Could be this is the day you knock one of those little dolls of Mistress Florence's on the floor or something. Then what?"

"Mistress Florence wouldn't take that as a way to—"

"No, Evie. We aren't going to take any chances today on getting on the bad side of any white folks." He reached out to tug her braid, but she pulled away from him, tears filling her eyes. They rolled past the stable, then the garden patch. Beyond it, Evie saw the home place wheat field, a soft, grassy green.

"Dry your eyes, now," Evie's father said gruffly. "I see your mama at the window watching for us."

Evie sat up straight and sniffled until the tears went away. Then she looked up at the house as they rolled closer. Pa was right. Mama was standing in the upstairs parlor, pressed up against the glass, her hands fluttering from her hair to her throat.

"Whoa up. Whoa," Pa sang out as he pulled the mares to a stop. He grinned up at the window and waved. Mama's answering smile was like sunshine. Then she disappeared. "Now you know she is headed down the stairs at a dead run," Pa said. "It will be about two more seconds before the door opens and they all come flying out at us." He was laughing, his smile wide and silly, like a boy's.

"There you are!" Mistress Florence was the first one to come through the door.

"Are we too early, Mistress?" Evie's father asked. He gave Mistress Florence a respectful little half bow, and she waved it away with a gesture.

"Too early? Of course not. You could have come an hour after moonrise and she would have been ready. I am so happy for you both," she said, turning back to look toward the house. "Well, I thought she was right behind me but she might be stuck in the hallway having a tizzy."

Pa laughed out loud, but Evie could hear the uneasiness in his voice. "I hope Marse James is ready with all the papers?"

Evie saw a dark look fly across Mistress Florence's face. It was there, then gone so quickly that she thought she might have imagined it. "I expect he has everything pretty well figured out, Griffin."

Evie stared at her father, willing him to turn and look at her, to relent and let her go inside, but he didn't even glance her way as he spoke to Mistress Florence in the low, amused voice he saved for white people.

"Well, then, maybe we ought to get on with things, if that's all right with you, Mistress."

Mistress Florence smiled. "Come right in. I have some raisin cookies in the kitchen for Evie and we can—"

"I thought she might just wait out here with the wagon," Pa interrupted quietly.

She frowned. "Whatever for?"

Pa ducked his head and spoke more to his shoes than to Mistress Florence. "It seemed to me that—"

"Nonsense. Evie is always welcome in this house, Griffin. As are you, and as Catherine will always be. I am hoping that you will come visit from time to time."

"Of course we will," Pa said. He stood still, waiting.

Mistress Florence made a gesture toward the house. "Let's go on in, then. James is in his study." When Evie hesitated, Mistress Florence reached out and took her hand. "Come on. The cookies won't stay warm all morning."

Evie let Mistress Florence lead her along like a toddle-baby, crossing the grass patch in front of the big house. As they got closer, Mama came down the steps.

"Oh, Griffin," Mama said, coming straight toward them. "Oh, Evie." She opened her mouth again, as though she wanted to say something else that just wouldn't pass her lips. Her eyes were red. She had been crying.

Marse James appeared at the top of the steps. "Why don't you all just come on in."

"Yessir," Pa said in his most careful, lowest voice. He had told Evie once that no white person could ever be a Negro's friend—not really—not as long as there was slavery. Not even the ones who tried their best. And Marse James didn't.

They all started walking toward the house. Evie looked down at Mistress Florence's hand on her own. She was chicken white, like the Kriegers. Evie could see veins through her fragile-looking skin. Evie's own skin looked warm and dark. Mistress Florence laced their fingers together as they walked toward the house. Evie stared at their hands, the fingers meshed: One dark, one light, one dark, one light . . . Mistress Florence squeezed her hand and leaned close to whisper, "Aren't you *excited?*"

Evie nodded. "Yes'm." She smiled at Mistress Florence's conspiratorial grin, then glanced away toward her parents. Pa had his arm around Mama, and she was leaning into his side. Her hands had stopped fluttering, but she looked wide-eyed and breathless.

Marse James held the door open. "We can go on up. I've got Quentin Marlboro up there, from next door."

"Yessir," Pa said. "A white man for to be our legal witness."

Evie heard the anger in her father's voice. She could tell that Marse James hadn't. She glanced around. Mama had. Her eyes flashed at Evie. One white man wasn't enough to sell a slave to her own husband. They needed *two* white men.

At the door, Evie pulled her hand free of Mistress Florence's. "I don't really want a cookie all that much, Mistress."

"You're probably too excited to eat. I would be." Mistress Florence turned to Mama. "Let the menfolks take care of all this. We could—"

"Please, Mistress," Mama said slowly. "I would like to be up there."

"I want to go, too," Evie breathed. It came out a little louder than she had meant it to.

"Oh, for heaven's sake," Marse James said. "Well, then, let's all go up. I have to get into town. I have a load of seed beans to pick up down on the levee."

"We sure wouldn't want to delay you none, Marse James," Mama said. "Make you late for the levee and those beans. Could be all the good ones'll be gone and only the wormy ones left for you."

Evie glanced at her mother's face. It was perfectly respectful. It was strange to listen to her parents talk like this, with two meanings to everything. If Marse James could have told the difference, he would have been insulted. Mama was telling him what she thought about her freedom being hurried for the sake of seed beans.

"That would be a shame," Pa put in politely.

"Let's go, let's go," Marse James said, gesturing emphatically to the stairs. He was smiling. Evie looked at him. Pa had said once that white people never really listened to black people. He was right, Evie thought.

Mistress Florence made a soft little sound of dismay. "What am I going to do without my darling Catherine?"

Mama reached out to pat Mistress Florence's cheek. "I'll just be in town. You'll know where to find me."

Marse James started up the stairs, with Pa right behind him. He shot Evie a sharp glance and she pretended not to see it. Mistress Florence had.

"Well, they don't much want us womenfolk up there, do they?" she whispered.

Mama laughed softly. "It looks like."

"Well, I think we should just go on up anyway. Come on." Mistress Florence gathered her skirts and started upstairs, the hoops brushing the wall.

Mama's face looked wan and pale like it did when she was feeling bad with one of her headaches. "I love you, Mama," Evie whispered. She wasn't sure why she had said it, but her mother's face told her it had been the right thing to say. Together, they started up the stairs.

CHAPTER NINE

Marse James was sitting behind his desk. He had his pen out, and an inkwell and blotting paper. There was a man Evie didn't know standing just behind Marse James's chair. He had a pinched face and weak, watery-looking eyes. He smiled, and his teeth were uneven and brownish.

"All right. Let's get this business out of the way, shall we?"

Pa made a small-voiced assent, and Evie tried to see his face, but he was turned away from her, facing Marse James.

"We have agreed on a price of seven hundred and fifty dollars. Is that correct?"

Evie felt her stomach clench. That was fifty more dollars than they had saved up. It was fifty dollars more than they could possibly pay today. What was he talking about?

"It was seven hundred even, Marse James." Pa

said it evenly, but Evie could see a little vein at the side of his neck pulsing beneath his skin. His eyes were narrowed, and he was staring at Marse James. "To my memory, anyhow," he added, his voice still very soft, very respectful. "I surely thought it was seven hundred even all this time."

"I thought it was seven hundred, too," Mama put in, and her voice was gentle, puzzled-sounding. "I am positive sure that's what you told me that first time we talked about this. The second time, we didn't talk about anything except the terms, that you'd take half then and let us—"

Mistress Florence cleared her throat. "Seven hundred seems adequate, doesn't it, James? I mean, we only paid three hundred for her, and she has hired out all this time without complaint or stinting."

"I seem to be overruled," Marse James said. He laughed, and the man behind his chair laughed with him. Evie looked away, trying not to catch anyone's eye, not even Mama's. She felt like she was going to explode into tears or tizzy-fits or something. Why were they laughing? What in the world was funny about anything?

"Well, then, let me just write this out," Marse James was saying. Evie turned back as he dipped the pen and began writing, scratching the steel nib across the paper. He had a fine, bold hand, and Evie forced herself to look vacant, blank, like a slave who thought writing was some kind of magic that made paper talk. Mama was staring at the paper as if it really were something conjured, something that might take wing before her eyes and turn into a dove to fly around the room, then out the door. Pa was standing quietly, slouched against the far end of the long desk. He was staring at the floor as though something interesting were taking place there. He had been so happy all morning. Now he looked dull and almost sad.

Evie heard Marse James begin to recite what he was writing. His voice was halting. He was speaking each word as he actually wrote it down.

"On this day of May 27, 1857, I, James Stevens of old Plank Road, St. Louis, Missouri, do herewith sell and convey one female slave, Catherine Stevens, known as Stevens's Catherine to those who are acquainted with her. She is a Negro woman of—"

Marse James broke off and looked up. Evie saw him furrow his brow. "How old are you, Catherine?"

Evie watched her mother take in a deep breath, then let it out. "I am about thirty, Marse James. Remember? They weren't quite sure at the old place, and we figured I was about nine or ten when you—"

"That's close enough, Catherine," he interrupted her, and dipped the pen again. Evie licked her lips. Her mouth and throat had gone dry. Her eyes felt strange, like fine dust had been thrown into them. Marse James cleared his throat, then began to write and recite again.

"...about thirty years of age. She is copper-colored, stout, and to my knowledge, healthy. She is a seamstress of considerable skill and good value. In consideration of her loyal service and longtime place in my household, I agree to accept a price of seven hundred dollars for her rcv'd in hand on this day, given by Griffin—"

He looked up again. "Griffin, I don't believe I ever knew your whole name. Do you go by William Peach's surname?"

Pa looked up. "I do. Griffin Peach. Evie, too. Since he freed us, we thought we owed him that much."

Marse James seemed to catch a little of the angry undercurrent in Pa's words. After all, Marse William had given them their freedom—Marse James was *selling* Mama's to her. Evie held her breath, afraid he had heard the insult. But then he smiled. "Of course. You owe him that and more, I am sure. He was a fine man and a good master."

Evie stood very still. She could see sparks of irritation in Marse James's eyes. His spine was stiff, his shoulders squared. There was a feeling of danger in the little room, a feeling that something awful might happen. Mama was right. Someday Pa's mouth might land them all in trouble. No one said anything for a moment, and Evie watched Marse James's face for a sign, but there was none. He seemed to be waiting politely for Pa to say something.

"Catherine and I have both been very fortunate to have fine men for masters," Pa said into the thickening silence.

Evie saw Marse James smile a little, then he let his posture soften. The sense of danger passed and she found she could breathe again, and Marse James went back to writing and reading aloud. The pen nib made tiny scratching sounds as he moved it across the paper.

". . . by Griffin Peach, a freedman emancipated by William Peach's will and testament, as purchase price in whole and total rcv'd in my hand on the above date. As witness to this said transaction, signs below Mr. Quentin Marlboro, long-standing subscriber and resident of St. Louis, his sign and seal in testimony hereafter affixed with my own."

He looked up once more. "Now you listen carefully, Griffin."

"Griffin Peach, in making his mark, understands and binds himself to this heretofore described transaction as final and renders all other obligations and promises null and void this 27th day of March, eighteen hundred and fifty seven."

He lifted the pen and set it down deliberately.

"That means that Catherine is not to come running back here looking for a meal or warm clothes if this emancipation scheme turns out to be bad judgment on both of your parts. I don't believe in any of this. Negro people need care and guidance, and you yourself know that most of them come to no good without it. I am doing it because my wife has asked me to and because I am fond of Catherine and know it is her wish. Are the terms clear to you?"

Evie watched her father nod, then, more slowly, her mother. Mistress Florence made a happy little sound like a woman at a wedding. "Well, then. You ought to get on with it, James," she said quietly, smiling brightly at Evie, then at her parents. Marse James picked up his pen again and dipped it in the inkwell. He signed his name to the paper, then drew his seal. When he was finished, he slid the paper so Quentin Marlboro could reach it easily. The witness smiled his crooked-toothed smile, then made a show of reading it over, his lips moving slightly. He wrote his bit, saying he was sign-ing in witness of what Marse James had written. Then he put his signature on the paper. It was big and frilly, with loops and spirals. His seal was equally elaborate.

Evie watched. Everyone in the room was star-ing as the two men made the document legal and binding. Both men had drawn the squiggly little cir-cles that white men called their seals beside their names. They looked like children's stick drawings in soft dirt.

"If you would just make your mark here, Griffin," Marse James said, his fingers lifting and falling like spider legs to spin the paper around. Evie watched her father take the pen. He held it awkwardly, as though he had never held one before in his life. Evie stared at the paper. Her father's handwriting was every bit as good as Marse James's. Maybe better. But Pa was rolling the pen in his fingers, leaning over. He hesitated, and Evie could see him trying not to read what was in front of his eyes. He made a shaky X, then turned the paper back around.

"I will write your name for you," Marse James said. "So that anyone reading this could identify the mark, too. He carefully printed "Griffin" on one side of the X and "Peach" on the other end so the name framed the mark like bookends.

Mr. Marlboro stepped from behind the desk. "If I won't be needed further, I will just be—"

"We thank you very much for coming on such short notice," Mistress Florence said quickly. Then she flushed and looked at Pa. "We had forgotten about needing a witness. I mean, we have been thinking about this for so long that we just thought it was going to happen all of its own and—"

"Florence, will you just show Mr. Quentin downstairs?" Marse James interrupted her. "Perhaps he would like a cup of coffee before he goes?"

"Perhaps," the man said, "if it isn't too much trouble." Pa moved back to let him pass, and Evie repositioned herself so Mistress Florence could maneuver her skirts back toward the door.

"No trouble at all, Mr. Marlboro," Mistress Florence said in a bright voice. "I'll just call Kizzy back from the dusting and have her fix up a fresh pot."

Evie heard Mistress Florence continue her pleasant chatter as they went down the stairs. Mr. Marlboro laughed at something she said. Marse William was looking down at the paper, sliding it back and forth across his polished wood desktop with a fingertip. Evie heard her mother take in a sharp breath and knew what she was thinking. Mistress Florence was the one they trusted some, not Marse James. And now she was gone.

"I have the money, Marse James," Pa said politely.

"That's good," Marse James said, looking up at them. His eyes slid from Pa, to Mama, to Evie. She looked down and away, unable to stand the pressure of his stare. He had light blue eyes, the color of winter skies. "Are you sure this is what you want, Catherine?"

Evie looked up instantly at the wheedling, odd tone of his voice. What was he doing?

"I am sure Griffin will be the first to admit that most freedmen in St. Louis are not doing very well. There is so much arguing over slavery, over what to do with people who don't really know how to take care of themselves. All the talk about sending shiploads of folk back to Liberia. . . ."

He trailed off, and Evie saw her father biting his lip. He had pulled the money from his pocket, and Evie knew all he wanted was to hand it to Marse James, grab the paper, and leave.

"Isn't that so, Griffin? Some are finding it too hard to pay for their rent and their food and clothes and everything else they need?"

"Yes, Marse James," Pa said reluctantly. "But some are making it just fine."

"Some," Marse James repeated. "A few, maybe. Not all. Not even most. And the ones who are rich almost don't count—they are all the French mulattoes from the Chouteaus' time. They've had family here since a hundred years ago."

Evie saw her mother sway a little on her feet and her right hand fluttered up to her face. "I want to go with my husband, Marse James," she said. "That's proper, isn't it? That a woman go with her husband and obey his wish?"

Evie watched her father take the money out of his pocket. He laid the folded bills carefully on the desk, then placed three gold pieces on top.

Marse James counted the money solemnly, slowly. He tucked it into the top drawer of his desk, then stood up, grunting a little with effort. "Well, then, I suppose that's all, isn't it?" He was smiling again, extending the paper in two fingers, holding it out for her father.

Pa took it from him and made a polite sound that wasn't quite words. Evie saw her mother turn to wobble toward the head of the stairs, her eyes flooding with tears. In two quick steps Pa had her elbow, steadying her. "Evie?"

"Coming, Pa," she answered, and turned to follow. She glanced back one last time. Marse James was still watching them, a smile on his face.

CHAPTER TEN

All the way down the drive they rode in silence except for Mama's little sniffling noises. Mistress Florence had hugged Mama and Evie so hard Evie could still smell her rose water. Evie hadn't hugged her back. Mama and Miss Florence had cried like sisters parting.

Evie stretched her legs, squirming to straighten her dress. Her shift had bunched up underneath, too. Nothing seemed right or comfortable. The sky looked too blue and the grass seemed too green and she felt like a stranger in her own skin.

Mama had turned around, riding almost backward for the first half mile, waving at Sam and Fanny and Kizzy, then looking back every few seconds until it was just plain impossible to see the house or even the tall trees that lined the drive. As they passed under a stand of cottonwoods that shaded the road where a little creek ran across it, Mama began to sniffle again. She was fighting her tears, Evie saw, but they wouldn't stop.

Evie looked aside, pretending not to notice. She could remember how scared she had been the first day she and Pa had come—freed—to St. Louis. And how much she had missed the folks at Marse William's at first. Everything had changed, and all at once. She had cried, too. She and Pa had ended up singing hymns most of the way into the city.

Evie patted Mama's shoulder, to show she understood, but it only made Mama cry a little louder. The wagon bumped and rose, then slammed down as they crossed a deep rut. This far up, Plank Road wasn't planked, or macadamized. It was a country road with farms and cottages on either side. Here and there Evie saw a big house with tended lawns and stately trees—the country estate of some wealthy family.

"I'm sorry, Griffin," Mama said. "I just—"

"We'll be fine, Catherine."

"But I know it's going to be hard," Mama said quietly. "I guess if I can work and you're working and Evie can help, then we ought to be all right." She wiped her eyes. "Shouldn't we be all right, Griffin?"

Pa nodded, smiling at her. "I told you, Catherine. Blacksmiths are gold in St. Louis now. Everything is building up and growing every which way. I can work as much as I can manage. And the pay is middling good. You'll work, and Evie already cleans for two women."

"I know, Griffin. It just feels so odd to be— away from there."

She made a gesture back toward Marse James's farm. Pa reached out and patted her hand. "You will get used to it, Catherine. And then you are going to wonder how you were ever content as a slave."

Mama nodded. "Nobody owns me, do they? It's a wonder I never thought to see."

Pa kissed her forehead, and she leaned against him. The wagon rattled along, and Evie looked out at the countryside, her heart relieved when Mama stopped crying. Pa was keeping Ginger at a quick trot with little taps of the whip.

"But it must cost so much for rent," Mama began. "I'll cook, but I have to eat something, too. And we will have to buy our own cloth for clothes and—"

"You aren't sorry we've done this, are you?"

There was a little pause, and Evie saw her mother exhale sharply, her shoulders slumping. "I am so very sorry, Griffin. I suppose I'm just . . ." Her hands fluttered up in a gesture that took in the scattered houses along Plank Road and the city of St. Louis ahead of them. "You have my paper?"

"Here," Pa said, pulling the bill of sale from his pocket. "And there's Evie's and my license receipts, too. You hold them."

Mama took the papers into her hands and held

them tightly. The bill of sale was a full sheet, and she started to fold it over the receipts, then gasped. "I've wrinkled it!" She sounded close to tears again.

"It's all right, Mama," Evie said quickly. "It'll smooth out fine."

Mama pressed the folded bill of sale against her skirt, then slipped the receipts into it and pinched the edge closed with her left thumb and forefinger. Pa fit the buggy whip back into the boot and reached out to take Mama's free hand. He held it for a long time, driving the mares more slowly, letting Ginger drop back into her lazy jog.

"The plantation where I grew up had whippings nearly every night," Pa said into the silence. "One little gal died, they whipped her so long. You've seen my back."

Mama nodded, somber, looking at him. His eyes were straight ahead, like he was talking to the road in front of them.

"I buried my mother at night, like we buried everyone at night. Because they wouldn't give anyone time off to have a funeral in the daytime."

Mama nodded again.

"Then Marse William bought me and brought me to Missouri when I was fourteen or so. He was good to me. He taught me and Evie to read. He set us free. And I still hate him."

Evie caught her breath. She had never heard Pa say anything like that before. She felt off balance again, like the world had shifted somehow and she was going to fall.

Mama tipped her head to one side, staring at Pa. "The Bible says that—"

"The Bible says what white men want it to say half the time," Pa interrupted.

"Pa, why would you hate Marse William?" Evie broke in. "He bought me from Marse James and he—"

"He bought me and left my two brothers to work and die in that cotton field. And you listen, Evie. He waited to free you and me until he didn't need us anymore. He was afraid of hell, more than anything. He knew he was sick."

"I will want to go to church, Griffin," Mama said firmly. She was staring at the side of his face.

"You are a free woman, Miss Catherine," Pa said, a smile twitching the corners of his mouth. "Nobody can stop you."

Mama frowned, then beamed at him, and he grinned back, turning to look into her eyes a second before he faced front again.

"Look there, Catherine," Pa said after a little while. "That's a beautiful little farm. Maybe someday we can have something like that."

"Marse James said we could never own anything. He said we'd have to have him to sign, or some white man."

"He likes to scare you," Pa said. "That law won't last. Too many folks hate slavery. A lot that don't hate it think it's bad for their businesses. The Irish hate it because it takes work from them. We might just get that farm someday."

Mama's eyes were dry now, and her face rapt as she imagined having her own farm to live on. She probably had never imagined it before in her life, Evie thought.

"We could go out West," Evie said. "Pa talked to a man about it. There are places in California and Oregon with land for whoever will build a cabin and work it—and almost no laws at all yet."

Mama's eyes widened, and Pa shot Evie a fierce look. "We were just talking, Catherine. We didn't mean anything by it."

"I should hope not," Mama breathed. She looked askance at Pa, and he caught her look out of the edge of his eye.

Evie saw him exhale sharply as he pulled the whip out of its boot and snapped it high above the mares' backs. "White folks have been going West for ten years. We see the wagons every day. They aren't all senseless little roosters like Marse James, are they?"

For a second, Mama looked outraged, but then

Pa chuckled. She laughed loud, then put both hands over her mouth to stop the sound. Pa reached up and pushed her hand away. "Go ahead. There's no one to tell you not to, is there?"

Mama shook her head, her eyes flooding up again. "You are right. He is the meanest little rooster of a man. Mistress Florence knows it, too, but what can she do with him?" She dabbed at her eyes.

"I cried the day we came to town, remember, Pa?" Evie said.

He nodded and smiled a little. "Now that you say it, I do recall. You were weepy halfway in to St. Louis."

"I'm sorry, Griffin," Mama said.

He put his arm around her shoulders. "You don't have to be sorry for anything. Not on this day."

Evie looked out over the road again, staring at the sun-dappled grass alongside it. It was beautiful. The land stretched out in front of them, dropping, then rising, then dropping again—like waves of earth lowering slowly toward the river. Evie could see the sun silvering the brown water even at this distance.

The mares clopped along, steadily bringing them closer to the city. At the tollgate, the man let them through without much talk again, looking side-long at Mama and the paper clutched in her hand.

"He thought this was our pass," Mama said once they were through, holding up the paper. "So he never even asked us."

"He's seen me before lots of times. I used to come in for Marse William sometimes twice a week. I don't know if he ever knew I was freed. He didn't ask us for slave passes on the way out, either."

"I always envied you coming to town," Mama said softly. "You got to know so much more than I did about everything." Evie saw that Mama's hands were trembling slightly.

"In a few weeks you'll know where all the colored groceries and all the theaters are, and how to parade up and down Main Street by the shop windows and—"

"Oh, stop now, Griffin." She turned to face him, and her eyes lit up. "I am so happy to be with you and Evie." She touched his cheek, then turned to take Evie's hand. Her eyes had filled up again, but the paper in her lap wasn't jiggling—her hands were steady now.

At the outskirts of town, Mama sat up straight, moving just a little ways away from Pa on the driver's bench. She watched the crowds on the sidewalks thicken and turned her head at every passing wagon.

"I have been here twice is all," she said to Pa. "Twice in thirty years. I always thought it was farther than this. Much farther."

He nodded. "Marse James doesn't come to town much himself, does he?"

"He often lets Sam do it for the family," Mama said. "Sam told me once that the markets here have fruit from Mexico and everywhere else there is."

Pa nodded. "That's true. I've seen mangoes, and other kinds I don't know a name for. There's lots of things brought in by steamboat. And now the railroad comes, too. I'll show you the new depot."

Mama nodded. "I want to see it. I want to see everything."

Her hands were completely relaxed now, except for the two fingers pinching her bill of sale, Evie saw. And she was smiling big and bright, like she always did when she was happy.

"You'll like our house, Mama," Evie said.

Pa nodded. "And I have a surprise there for you."

Mama's smile broadened. "Your father is a good man," Mama said to Evie, still smiling like sunshine. "I ever tell you that?"

"You have, Mama," Evie said. She was feeling dizzy-headed and excited again, and it felt good. Mama was here with them. They wouldn't have to leave her tonight, or any other night. They could all be together forever now.

CHAPTER ELEVEN

"Look!" Mama breathed. She was pointing to a tall building on the corner of Tenth Street. It had curving stonework that jutted out of the brick walls just beneath the roofline. "Look how that's carved."

"Wait until you see the new courthouse they're building," Pa was saying. "It has more stone ornaments than a plantation hearth mantle."

Mama's eyes went wide as she turned back around. "All big like that?"

"Bigger," Pa said, but Mama was already looking elsewhere, her head moving back and forth, her eyes flickering from one thing to the next. Pa got Ginger and Lucky back into a trot and kept them there, even though it jolted them all when the wheels jounced across the ruts.

Pa gestured to draw Mama's attention to the bustle of wagons and omnibuses that streamed down Plank Road. "Plank Road's name changes to

Olive Street somewhere in here. Remember that if you ask directions. That's what the town folk mostly call it."

"Olive Street." Mama repeated it like it was a solemn oath.

Pa nodded. "And this is one of the better stretches this time of day. From the wharves on the levee up to Fifth or Sixth, it can get crowded. Sometimes the wagons get so thick, they all have to stop—no one can move any direction."

Mama caught her breath. "They all just . . . stop?" She looked amazed, then a heavy-set mulatto woman in a bright green dress caught her eye and she jutted out her chin. "Look at that hat. Any bigger, it'd tip her over."

Pa chuckled and tilted his head, indicating the opposite side of the street. There, a beautiful Negro woman was dressed in so many crinolines that her skirt bobbed like a cork when she walked. Mama huffed again. "I will be glad when that fashion passes. And hoops."

Pa nodded and smiled at Evie over Mama's head. "I do believe your mama is going to like St. Louis. We'll have to show her that little tree from China on the way home."

"Town sure has more goings-on than the farm," Mama said. "What do you mean, a tree from China?"

Pa laughed aloud this time. He explained about trying to buy a Chinese tree, then deciding on an apple tree instead.

Mama smiled at him, then turned to grin at Evie. "You both sure do know me. I'd love to *see* the one from China, though. Imagine, it came all that way on a ship, over the water. That's what Mistress Florence said about the silk she ordered in—said it came from the other side of the world."

Mama started making little sounds of delight as they went through town. Pa drove her past the courthouse and circled once, acting like one of the carriage drivers who hired out to rich folks from the East. He talked like a tour guide, too, pointing at the St. Louis Theater on Pine between Third and Fourth, then at Wood's Theater a little farther down. "There's the new G. Conzelman's paperhanging and upholstery store," he said, gesturing. "I know a man whose wife works there. She sews up chair cushions and such."

Mama twisted around on the bench. "Maybe I could do that."

Pa smiled, pulling the mares in a wide arc. "Maybe. Look, there's the courthouse again. From this side you can see the new wing better." Mama pulled in a sharp breath and stared at the big brick and stone building. "They have been working on it going on ten years now, I'm told," Pa said. He guided the mares around the last corner, and they were headed straight toward the river again on Chestnut Street. "There's Center Market." He pointed.

Mama squinted, shading her eyes with her right hand, her left still pinching their papers tightly in her lap. "Everything is so *big*."

Evie smiled, listening to them. The sun was warm. All around them were the sharp, busy sounds of the city: turning wheels and hooves on the macadam, whips cracking and crowds talking. From the levee came steamboat whistles and the clanging of ironworks.

Pa turned south down Seventh and drove almost all the way down to Rutgers, showing Mama the fancy houses in that neighborhood. "My word and heaven above," Mama said, staring at the widow Pelagrie's mansion. "Who lives there?"

"A woman who used to be a slave," Pa told her, smiling. "The widow of a man of color who had a wealthy father. They inherited a fortune. At least that's what Willis Jackson says."

"Who is Willis Jackson?" Mama asked.

Evie sat forward. "A steamboat barber who brings his horse to Pa to shoe."

"He's free like us," Pa said. "His brother is a slave, still, owned by the man Willis works for."

Mama nodded thoughtfully. "It might take me

awhile to understand much about this life in the city."

"But you will," Pa said.

They kissed, quickly, then faced front again. Pa pulled the reins and headed east on Rutgers Street, downhill toward the river. "I'll take us back up Main so you can get a look at some of the shops and warehouses, then we'll show you the China tree. And then I want to get on home. I want there to be daylight left so that you can really see the place."

All the way up Main Street, Mama sighed and hummed over the stores. In one doorway, a tall, black-haired, black-suited man stood in the center of a little crowd of listeners. There was a strong odor of camphor in the air. The man held forth the little glass bottle for a woman to sniff. She wrinkled her nose, and the crowd laughed. "That's the strength of the tincture," the man said proudly.

Without meaning to, Evie read the sign behind him. DR. JAMES C. AYER, PRACTICAL AND ANALYTICAL CHEMIST. She wasn't sure what "analytical chemist" meant, but she knew he was selling medicines and tonics of some kind. She had seen his notices in the *Weekly Missouri Democrat* many times. Willis brought the old copies from the steamboat saloon sometimes, hiding them under his coat.

Mama was grinning like a girl. She pointed at a stand of bright parasols, then at a rack of shawls hung out to attract passersby. When she saw a stand with fruit piled in colorful bins she sighed aloud, still smiling. "It's beautiful."

The din of the crowds on Main Street bothered Evie less than usual, and she knew it was because Mama was having so much fun seeing everything for the first time like this. It was impossible not to smile at her astonishment. They passed E. G. Tuttle Millinery Goods and saw a sign in the window. Mama lowered her voice. "What's it say?"

Evie leaned close. "It says, 'Bonnets! Bonnets! Bonnets!' That's what their newspaper ad has said lately, too. I guess they got a shipment of them in from somewhere."

"Oh, look, you can see them in the window," Mama cried out. She stretched up, trying to get a better view. "How can there be that many bonnets in the whole world?"

Evie shook her head. "I don't know, Mama," she said, forcing herself to look serious. "But there must be some way, because there they are!"

Pa glanced around, then spoke. "I saw an ad in the *Missouri Republican* yesterday that said Brown & Company had got in $250,000 worth of dressmaker's cloth and notions. It said they'd just received 15,000 parasols."

"Parasols," Mama echoed. "And cloths? Yard

goods?" Her voice was dreamy. Evie knew she was imagining the bolts of linen, velvet, alpaca, and heavy moleskin. And soft woolen cassimere. Mama loved good cassimere.

Pa pulled the team in to wait for a big dray loaded with lumber to pass before he turned onto Locust Street. Evie looked up the block, hoping her mother wouldn't notice the slave traders' establishment as they went past it.

"There!" Evie said, spotting the placard in front of the nursery warehouse. "There it is, Pa!" She pointed so that Mama would look down the block, too, and her father caught her eye with an approving little nod.

"I see it." He angled Ginger and Lucky toward the door, swinging them in close so the wagon was well over to that side of the street. They climbed down off the bench, Mama shifting the folded bill of sale from one hand to the other as she bent to brush at a spattering of dust on the front of her skirt. Evie looked past her, at the wall full of tacked-up broadsides. It was hard not to read them. The lettering was big, the reward figures in bold black ink.

"Hey!"

Evie glanced up at the sudden shout.

"What makes you think you can hurt my brother like that and get away with it?"

Liam Maloney was coming toward them. Sean

was a step or two back, with Paddy and Drew strung out behind him—all but Terrence. Evie saw her father turn, heard her mother's quick breath, then everything seemed to happen so fast, it was like a dream.

Liam was yelling into her father's face, his stance wide, his shoulders squared. Pa was trying to tell him that he hadn't done anything at all to Terrence, but Liam couldn't hear anything over the sound of his own voice. Sean stood wild-eyed, hands on hips, Drew and Paddy beside him.

Pa held up both hands. "I didn't do—"

"Terrence told us all that you did," Liam shouted. He looked at Sean, who nodded emphatically. There was a chorus of shouts from Paddy and Drew. A few people slowed their step, watching.

"Darkies like you should be sold down the river," Liam spat. His body was tense with fury—he was shaking as he spoke.

"I am a free man," Pa said, his voice uneven. People were stopping to watch now, and he stepped back from Liam, rounding his shoulders, ducking his head. "You know me, Liam. We all have papers—"

"These are runaways from Virginia," Liam shouted. "They stole that wagon from my father!"

He pointed at the mares, and Evie took a step

backward, astounded at his lies. But she could see belief in the faces around them. People were used to runaways being caught here—on their way to Illinois.

"We do have papers!"

Evie whirled to see Mama holding out the bill of sale she had clutched so tightly all day. Their license receipts were folded inside it.

"No, Catherine!" Pa roared, but it was too late. Liam snatched the papers away, spinning to thrust them at Sean with a single word. "Run!"

Evie stood, transfixed, as Liam tipped back his head and began shouting loudly enough for the whole street to hear. "Help! Help us! Please!"

Evie felt sick, as though someone had tilted the world again and she could only fight for her balance. Her father's ferocious grip on her shoulder brought her back to her senses. "Go now, Evie," he rasped into her ear. "Slip away and get home. Get our emancipation papers." He pushed her to one side and she stumbled, then found her feet.

An instant later she was stepping back, sliding between people who were staring, puzzled at the commotion. Her breath short and quick, her heart aching, Evie forced herself to walk, head down, without looking back. She found a narrow opening between buildings and dodged into it.

"Runaways!" she heard Liam shout as she turned the corner. "Help us. These are runaways!"

Within a minute the sound of Liam's shouting had faded, and she could hear only the drumming of her own heart. Evie pulled her dress straight and wiped her eyes. Everything depended on her now. Everything.

CHAPTER TWELVE

Evie stood still, terrified that the commotion would follow her, that in seconds there would be shouts and the sound of heavy footsteps from Locust Street. But nothing happened. She clenched her fists and forced herself to peek back around the corner.

It was impossible to see Pa or Mama—there was a tight crowd around them now. But people were vying to be heard.

"Get them up to the courthouse," a deep voice suggested.

"Courthouse is closed for the day," another man answered.

"Take them down to Lynch's, then. Save time later if that's where they belong anyway." That was a woman's voice.

"Lynch'll feed them tonight and make sure they don't get to the ferry."

"Yeah. He's got them bars on the windows around back. They won't go nowhere."

Evie closed her eyes. She pressed herself close to the side of the building as a murmur of assent rose from the crowd.

"Where'd the gal go?" someone asked suddenly. "Didn't they have a little gal with them, maybe ten or twelve?"

"Where is she?" It was Liam, clear and loud above everyone else.

"I saw her go before I knew what the matter was." That was the deep voice again. "She's probably half a mile away by now."

Evie leaned forward until she could see him. He was a big man with silver whiskers framing his long, pale face. He pointed vaguely across the street. Good. He thought she'd gone that way.

"She's young and she'll be scared," another man said. "I'll drive on up to the upper ferry, tell them to be on the lookout for a little runaway trying to get over to Illinois free soil."

"I'll go tell the Spruce Street ferryman," another man put in. He had pock-scarred skin, and long dark hair tied back in a thong.

Evie knew she should go, but she was scared to move, afraid that the instant she left the comforting solidness of the wall everything would collapse—

someone would see her and give chase. Evie shivered, forcing herself to straighten up, then to push back from the wall and turn up the narrow path. Heart galloping, knees trembling, she began to walk.

Liam and Sean would know where she was heading—but they probably wouldn't tell anyone else. If they admitted they lived across the street from her, they would have to explain why they didn't know her father was a freedman—why they acted as though he was a stranger to them.

But that didn't mean they wouldn't try to find her, try to stop her from getting the papers back to her father if they understood that was what she intended to do. Had Liam overheard her father? She didn't think he had—Pa had been cautious, and his voice hadn't been much above a whisper. But Liam might figure out what her running meant.

Evie hurried up the narrow passage between buildings. She forced herself to keep putting one foot in front of the other, her breathing quick and her thoughts spinning like tops on hard dirt as she glanced back down the narrow canyon between the brick walls. She swallowed, suddenly remembering her father's stories about bloodhounds in North Carolina. Most dogs barked when they were giving chase, Pa had said, but the bloodhounds were silent. And they could follow human scent through high grass and powder dust and along creeks. She remembered more than that, too—his stories of whippings that left slaves dying, or so badly hurt they could never recover. His own scars were awful, long and pale.

Evie slowed a little as she came out into the back alley that separated the buildings facing Locust from the ones that fronted on Vine Street. It was empty except for a few children digging through a trash barrel. Evie sprinted across the open space, her eyes scanning the backs of the buildings. Finally she spotted another narrow opening on the far side of a brick building with an enormous smokestack rising from its roof. This one was so tight that her shoulders brushed the walls on either side as she went.

Evie glanced behind herself every few seconds, but she saw only the far end of the passage, an empty rectangle of late afternoon daylight. She made herself slow down a little once she emerged from the little pathway onto Vine Street. She tried to stop breathing hard, tried to look calm as she searched the faces of the crowd. Most of them didn't look at her. Those who did seemed not to notice her fear. She stepped onto the sidewalk, easing herself to the outside so that she could step off into the street if a white person needed more room. The last thing she needed now was for someone to think she was impudent and didn't know her place.

How could I not know? Evie thought. How could any person of color not know? The lesson was taught every day. Her mother and father were being taken to a slave trader's pens, unable to get anyone to believe the simple truth—that they were free.

Trying to be invisible, her thoughts in a wrenching tumble, Evie made her way toward the end of the block. At the corner, she looked south down Second Street—back toward Locust—and caught her lower lip between her teeth again, cautious. Had any of the people walking toward her been in the crowd around her parents? Had any of them seen her run? She stepped off the curb—the sidewalk was high here—and started across.

Evie's palms were sweating with fear, but no one called out, no one seemed to notice her at all. She crossed the street, weaving her way through the wagons and carriages. She kept her eyes down and her pace fast, and tried hard to look like she was just in a hurry—not desperate.

As Evie followed Vine to Third Street, then uphill to Fourth, the late afternoon crowds were thinning out a little. She tried not to keep looking behind herself, but it was impossible. She expected every second to hear Liam's voice, or running footsteps. When a grocery driver shouted at his mules, she spun around before she could stop herself, then turned back and almost ran, her head down.

"Oh, dear, look where you're going!" The voice was high and shrill.

Evie raised her eyes, but it was too late. She could not stop before she had run into a tall white woman. She was pretty, with rosy cheeks, and wore an elaborate walking costume of blue and violet. She stared at Evie. "You are certainly in a hurry." She dabbed at her forehead with a white linen handkerchief, then slipped it back inside the bodice of her dress.

Evie shook her head, fighting to stay calm. "I apologize. I just have to get home now, Mistress. Excuse me, please."

"I certainly don't mean to detain you, dear," the woman said, laughing a little. "Is something wrong?" The woman scrutinized Evie's face. "Maybe I could help."

Evie stared up at her, unable to stop her heart from rising with hope. If this woman was an abolitionist, maybe she *could* help. Evie started to speak, but caution closed her lips. If the woman *wasn't* an abolitionist, asking her for help could be dangerous. And Evie knew she could not afford to lose even a second.

"Thank you." Evie swallowed and squared her shoulders. "But nothing is wrong, Mistress." She said it clearly and evenly, then managed a little false smile. "I just have to get on home now. I can't be out after dusk without a pass."

The woman smiled back at her and patted her cheek. "All right, then. You be a good girl, now."

Evie nodded. The woman went past, her wide skirts sweeping the planks. Evie stood still for a few seconds, just long enough to let the woman disappear into the crowd. Then she began to walk, her legs aching and her heart thudding as she headed north again.

Fourth Street ran along the crest of a low ridge, high enough that Evie could see the river as she crossed Washington Street, then Green. Just as she stepped off the sidewalk down to the rutted surface of Morgan Street, she heard some shouting behind her.

Without even glancing back, Evie ran, darting sideways through a group of women who strolled with folded parasols. One of them screamed when Evie ran past, a short, clipped little sound. The other women laughed at their startled companion and called good-natured protests after Evie. Then she was too far past them to hear or see more.

Where Fourth Street ended, Evie looked west down Franklin Street, then decided impulsively to turn right onto Cherry Street instead. She zigzagged through the people on the street, slowing her pace a little so no one would stare at her, trying to calm down enough to think. Home seemed so far away. But somehow, she had to get their emancipation papers out from under the loose plank beneath her cot. She needed to get her mother's bill of sale back, too. Would Sean just run home? Would he hide it somewhere?

A cold prickle of fear crawled across her skin and nearly made her stumble. Would Sean tear the paper up? Were they that cruel? Even if Marse James was willing to replace it, it'd take too long to go tell him, then come back. Her mother could be on a steamboat headed for the Deep South by the time Marse James even knew something was amiss. And if Mama was already sold South, what difference could he make?

Evie pulled in a shuddering breath. She wanted to run so badly, but the sea of faces kept her striding along, walking as fast as she could. She had to stay calm. She had to *think*. The shouting might not have had anything to do with her—and she had lost precious time turning east.

At the next corner—Main Street—Evie turned north toward home again. Here, where the streets were thronged with people, it'd be harder for anyone to spot her.

Evie worked her way around a fat man wearing a butcher's apron around his waist. The white cotton was stained in irregular red and brown patches, stiff with old blood. He was whistling. A little farther on, Evie ran a few steps to dart in front of two Catholic Sisters walking slowly side by side. For an instant, Evie thought about asking the nuns for help. But not all of them were abolitionists, she knew. Fiona had told her that some of the Sisters thought the Church should stay out of the argument altogether.

Evie glanced back at the nuns. Their faces seemed clear and kind—but it was too great a risk. If anyone caught her now, her father might not be able to prove his freedman state if he was taken to court. *If.* It was possible they would just sell him down South, too—especially if he did anything foolish or tried to fight back. Evie had heard stories. And Mama would have only her word. Evie felt sick. How could all this have happened so fast?

Evie looked down just in time to see some broken

glass, feeling one sharp prick in the bottom of her left foot. She took a few more steps, hoping the pain would subside. It did. She might have a tiny cut, but the glass hadn't stuck into her callused sole.

Evie thought about trying to spot a Negro wagoner to ask for a ride, but the truth was she could walk faster than the wagons were moving now. The sun was low in the sky. In an hour, it'd be dusky. The streets were filling up with wagons—everyone was starting to head home for the night.

At the corner of Biddle Street, Evie decided to zigzag once more, this time heading west for a few blocks before she turned northward again. She was about halfway around the corner when she heard a boy shout, "There she is!"

Through the crowd, Evie caught a glimpse of Liam's face. It took her a moment to realize he was sitting in the wagon—driving Lucky and Ginger through the tight maze of wagons and merchandise and people. His brothers were with him, crowded onto the bench. Evie whirled and began to run again.

She raced along, leaping into the street to get around an elderly white man with a cane, then leaping back up onto the sidewalk when a Lemp's Lagerbier wagon rumbled past, the huge barrels swaying like tree trunks in a storm. She knew her only chance was now, right here, where the wagons choked the streets and she could outrun and out-maneuver them.

She dodged a stack of crates taller than she was, then crossed the street at a dead run. She could hear steamboat whistles, and the smell of the muddy river was strong. The street was filled with wagons and carriages, creeping along.

Evie ducked behind a stalled carriage, almost knocking down a boy about her own age. His dark blue stiff-collared jacket told her he was the foot-man. "I'm sorry," Evie rasped.

He looked at her wide-eyed. "Are you the run-away?"

Evie caught her breath, then shook her head. "They took my parents away. They're free, both of them. But some boys . . ."

"Are you free?" The boy's dark eyes were full of feelings—admiration, wonder, envy.

Evie took in a breath. "Who said there was a runaway?"

"Someone was shouting it earlier, that we were to look out for one—a girl. I won't tell. And nobody is in there—" He tapped on the side of the closed carriage. "We just let them off about two blocks down."

Evie's eyes strayed to the carriage, sliding

along its polished fenders. The boy understood her thought instantly. "Go ahead. Get in. Just open the door easy and old Clander won't even look round. We go straight up Main to the upper ferry, then down Wright to—"

"Tap on the fender when we cross Benton," Evie interrupted.

"I'll do better than that," the boy said. "You wait and see." He put one foot up on the little platform where he would ride, motioning her forward. She glanced back. The driver behind them was dozing on his bench.

The carriage rolled a little, then stopped. Evie darted up alongside it, half crouched, and pulled the door open. She hitched herself up onto the carriage step, then all the way in onto the seat. She pulled the door closed, instantly leaning back to hide herself.

Evie held her breath. Had that taken a few seconds, or a few hours? Time seemed to be stretching and shrinking like pulled taffy. No one shouted. There were no rushing footsteps. She exhaled slowly, waiting, grateful beyond words to the boy. Even with Ginger feeling spunky and happy about going home, the two old mares were no match for the team that pulled this carriage.

With a sudden lurch, the carriage started

forward. Evie could hear the horses' shoes striking the gravelly road surface and she could imagine them, manes streaming, tails like flags, their hooves snapping up and down, as they trotted along. Evie slid down the plush, tufted upholstery and lay down on the velvet seat, staring at the black carriage top, daring to hope.

CHAPTER THIRTEEN

On the curve where the streets followed the line of the river past Labeaume Street, Evie dared to sit up, scrooching up against the back of the seat. The carriage was still rolling along smartly, the fine horses making good time on the hard-surfaced street. Evie wanted, more than anything, to lean out the window and look back down Main Street, but she knew it would be foolish—worse than foolish. She turned around on the seat, running her hand across the soft velvet upholstery. She had never ridden in a carriage before. She knew she was not likely to again.

She heard the ferry bell and twisted around, surprised. The horses really were going fast. They would be crossing Benton in less than a block. Evie put her hand on the door latch, the nickeled brass cool against her sweaty palm, and waited. She wasn't sure what the boy was going to do, but she had no choice. She had to trust him.

There was a sudden sharp, loud shout. Evie was startled into slumping down in the seat. An instant later, the carriage slowed, and Evie could hear the scrape of the brake on the wheels. The second the horses came to a stop, Evie heard an old man shouting, "Randall? Are you all right, boy?"

"I'm over here," the answering shout came. "I think I hurt my ankle."

Evie peeked out. Randall saw her and gave a vague nod, limping, veering toward the other side of the carriage. Evie ducked back, counted to three, then looked again and caught a last glimpse of the driver as he walked alongside Randall, both of them disappearing around the far side of the carriage. She could hear them talking as she slid out the door, closing it soundlessly before she glanced up and down the street. No one was near enough to have seen her get out.

She walked close alongside the carriage to the horses' rumps, then angled away a little so that she wouldn't startle them as she passed. She glanced back twice, hoping to give Randall a little wave or some sign of her gratitude, but he kept the driver on the far side of the carriage, giving her plenty of time to get a block or more ahead before the carriage began to move again.

Evie turned down Warren Street, passing each

familiar house, every familiar tree, with rising spirits. She sprinted the last little way, running up the porch steps. She did not pause, but ran through the main room and flung open her bedroom door.

The plank came up easily as it always did, and Evie fished out her diary with shaking hands. The blue cloth cover was as welcome as the face of a friend. She set it on the floor beside herself, then leaned forward again, lying on her belly to reach down into the secret place.

Their emancipation papers were in a flat cigar box and Evie pulled it out, rocking back on her heels to get her diary. She returned it to the hiding hole, then replaced the plank and sat back. This would free Pa—and then they could go to court to prove they had their freedmen's licenses if they had to. But what about her mother? Evie bit at her lip and tasted blood.

"What are you doing?" The voice so startled Evie that she leaped to her feet, spinning around, the box clutched beneath her arm. Terrence stood in the doorway, his face swollen and his right eye bruised black beneath its cut.

Evie was seized with rage. "How could you tell your brother that my father hurt you? You know that's a lie. Pa *helped* you."

Terrence swayed on his feet, shifting his weight back and forth. "I didn't. Liam made it up.

He said he would tell our father I wasn't in school if I tattled."

"If you told the truth?"

Terrence nodded. "I didn't make up the lie, though. Liam did—to get back at you for scaring us. . . ." Terrence cupped his hands to his mouth and made a good imitation of Evie's "haint" sound. Then he smiled crookedly, wincing when the smile hurt his swollen face. "I was scared."

"I'm sorry," Evie said. "I meant it for Sean and Liam, mostly."

Terrence looked down at his worn-out shoes, his lanky hair falling over his forehead. "If you tell them I told you, they'll—"

"I won't," Evie promised. "I have to go now. You'd better go home or—"

"Sean said I better not tell anything if I saw you first," Terrence said.

Evie had already taken one step toward the door. She froze, midstride, then looked back at him. "Sean? Is he home now?"

Terrence nodded, touching his swollen cheek. "But Liam isn't. Nor Paddy nor Drew. Do you know where they are?"

Evie shook her head. "They're coming. They stole our wagon and the mares. They probably think that if we are all sold South, they can just figure a way to keep them." She paused, watching him absorb what she had said. "Where's Sean?" Evie asked, trying to keep her voice patient and kind. Terrence looked like a cornered rabbit, ready to run.

"He was in the garden last I saw, digging. Do you want to talk to him?"

Evie shook her head. "Will you show me where?"

Terrence looked up at her sidelong. "Why?"

Evie hesitated, then decided to tell the truth. "Maybe," she said slowly, "maybe he was burying our papers." She stared into Terrence's pale little face and explained what had happened. "I know you're afraid of your brothers, but if I don't get them back, my mother could be sold somewhere and then I'll never see her again. Please, Terrence. Oh, God, *please*, Terrence."

Terrence was silent, and Evie felt her throat tighten. Then he spoke. "Fiona says you're nice to her." Without saying anything else he led her out the door and across the yard. As she walked, Evie rolled up the emancipation document. Then she slipped the tight little roll of paper into the bodice of her dress, inside her chemise, next to her skin. The drawstring at her waist held it safe.

"There."

Terrence was pointing. Sean had dug a number

of holes near his mother's potato patch. Evie clawed at the soft earth in the first one. It was shallow, and empty. By the third hole, she was beginning to despair. Had he just done this to fool Terrence so that he could fool her, too? Or had he been looking for softer dirt? She refilled and smoothed each hole—she wouldn't let Sean know she had fallen for his trick, if that's what it was.

The fourth hole was deeper, and Evie scooped the soil with both hands. Finally, a tiny corner of paper showed, and Evie cried out with joy. Terrence stepped out of the trees to smile at her.

The paper was only a little soiled when Evie pulled it free of the dry dirt. She filled the hole again and smoothed it as she had the others.

Once she was safely hidden by the cottonwood trees, Evie thanked Terrence. He smiled again, his poor swollen cheek pink and painful looking. "Can I hide in your stable when Liam comes home?"

Evie touched his hair. It was warm from the late sun. "I'll tell Pa. You can hide there whenever you want."

"Get up! Come on! Get up!"

Evie looked up. Liam and his brothers were coming up the road at a fast trot. As fast a trot as Ginger would allow, anyway. Liam was standing on the footrest, flicking the reins up and down so hard that Evie could hear the leather pop. He either didn't know there was a whip, or he had lost it. Either way, Evie was glad for the mares.

"I have to go now," she told Terrence. "Take care of the mares later if you can. There's hay in the stable and water buckets in their stalls."

"I know how to unharness. My Granfer taught me," Terrence told her. "Be careful, Evie."

She nodded, tears welling up in her eyes. "I'll be home today or tomorrow," Evie said. "I hope," she added, just in case she couldn't make it true.

Terrence nodded, then stepped back into the trees. "I won't tell anyone you came here," he promised.

Evie kissed his forehead and started off in the direction the wagon had come from. The instant she was around the corner of Warren onto Second Street, she began to run. By the time Liam gave up waiting for her, it would be too late for him to stop her. Evie pulled in a deep breath. She was tired and hungry, but she knew it didn't matter. She had to run.

CHAPTER FOURTEEN

Evie's bare feet made soft slapping sounds in the dust along the road as she ran. The sound of her own breathing seemed louder than anything around her—even the whistles of the steamboats as they maneuvered into the docks for the night or splashed out onto the wide river to start a new journey.

By the time Evie had reached Labeaume Street, the last fiery curve of the sun was disappearing below the blue hills on the horizon west of town. The Mississippi always looked strange to Evie right at sundown, the water reddened by the rosy light.

Evie ran a long time, looking around at first, then with her head down, breathing hard, watching the roadway for broken glass or sharp rocks. A few wagons passed, but no one bothered her. For a little while longer, they probably wouldn't—she looked like she was running to get home before night fell.

Crossing Mulanphy Street she saw a white man staring at her from a wagon stopped by the side of the road. She slowed immediately and shook her head as she came toward him, trying to look embarrassed, not scared.

"I better hurry home now, sure enough!" Evie managed to say as she passed him, keeping her voice low and musical like Pa did when he had to talk to white people he didn't know or couldn't figure.

His look of suspicion changed into a smile. "You surely better. You live close?"

"Close enough, Marse," Evie said without slowing her step. "If I hurry." He smiled and nodded, then looked back at the sunset. Anyone could stop her, Evie knew. And after it was truly dark someone probably would. Once there were low hanging branches to conceal her from the man in the wagon, she started running again.

Locust Street was nearly deserted when Evie finally rounded the corner, her breath painful, her legs aching. She ran as far as the warehouse where they had seen the China tree, then slowed, her eyes fixed on the next block.

There was a light on in Lynch's office. Was that usual? She had no way of knowing. She knew she should hurry, but fear weighed her step and slowed her down. She dragged in one long breath after another, staring at the gold-yellow of the bright windows.

Lynch's. Just the name of the place was enough to make her feel a fear that seemed to settle around her bones and in her heart. Negroes who ended up at a slave trader's were already worse off than most. Sometimes a slave was sold to a neighbor, or a relative—someone the master thought would be kind and good. Being sold through a dealer, there little chance of that. Or more than the slightest chance of families staying together.

Evie touched the rolled-up papers inside her chemise, reassuring herself, trying to steady her breathing. The barred windows were around the back of Lynch's building, the man had said. Evie forced herself to walk, keeping her eyes moving, ready to run. She would just hand Pa the papers through the window bars.

"In a few minutes, this will be over," Evie whispered to herself, trying to drown out the hammer-pound of her heart as she slid close to Lynch's side wall and followed it to the back of the building. She stopped close to the barred window and pulled in a shivery breath.

"Pa?"

There was no answer.

"Pa? Mama?"

There was only silence.

"Pa? Are you in there?"

"They took a man named Peach and his wife down below."

The voice was a harsh whisper.

"Below?" Evie whispered back, her scalp prickling with fear.

"Underground," the voice rasped. "They have rooms down there for runaways."

"How can I get down there?" Evie whispered.

There was a pause. Then a short, pained laugh from behind the bars. "Through the front door, honey. That's the only way."

Evie stepped back, a grating fear weakening her legs, her will. She walked unsteadily back to the street and crossed quickly, afraid every second that someone would see her. At the end of the block, the lamplighter was beginning his rounds. Evie stopped opposite Lynch's front entry and stared.

The light in the office was already burning—a fancy gas lamp, Evie saw. And there were three white men reading newspapers by its yellowish glow. One had his feet up on his desk, leaning back in his chair. Evie stared at them. Could she trust any of them?

Evie swallowed, staring at their faces. One was older than the other two. Maybe he would be more fair, more likely to see the simple justice in letting her parents go. Maybe he would let them leave tonight, after he had seen their papers.

Evie lifted her head and started across the street, imagining herself holding out the precious papers, letting go of her end as the man's fingers closed on the other. She almost stumbled as her imagination supplied an image of Sean grabbing her mother's bill of sale and running. What was to keep these men from taking the papers, then denying that they had ever seen them? These men were slave traders. *Slave traders.*

Evie shuddered and stopped, her bare feet stinging from her long run, her heartbeat and breath quick and frightened again. She stared into the lit window for a moment. There was no choice. She had to climb those steps.

Evie swallowed. She felt hot all over, then shivered, as though she had a fever. Her feet made almost no sound on the stairs, and the open office door allowed her to pass inside in complete silence. All three men continued reading their newspapers— the older man was chewing a stem of grass, or maybe parsley from supper. Behind him a letter was posted on the wall. "Excuse me?" Evie said hoarsely.

All three men jumped. The oldest man recovered himself first. "What do you want?"

"You have my parents here," Evie said.

One of the younger men got up. "Well, well. The

Kerry Patch kids were right. There was a third one."

"Can you take me to my parents, please, Marse?" Evie said in a low voice. She could not keep the tremor out.

"I suppose we can oblige," the older man said. Now that he was looking at her, Evie could see how hard and cold his eyes were. He stood and slipped behind her. She heard the door close. Thank God she had not decided to trust him—or any of them. Behind the desk, affixed to the wall, was a paper with big bold handwriting on it. Evie pretended to stare blankly as she read it, waiting.

RULES
No Charge less that One Dollar

ALL NEGROES ENTRUSTED TO MY CARE FOR SALE OR OTHERWISE. MUST BE AT THE RISK OF THE OWNERS.

A CHARGE OF 37 1/2 CENTS WILL BE MADE PER DAY FOR BOARD OF NEGROES, 5 & 1/2 PER CENT ON ALL SALES OF SLAVES.

MY USUAL CARE WILL BE TAKEN TO AVOID ESCAPES OR ACCIDENTS, BUT WILL NOT BE MADE RESPONSIBLE SHOULD THEY OCCUR.

I ONLY PROMISE TO GIVE THE SAME PROTECTION TO OTHER NEGROES THAT I DO TO MY OWN. I BAR ALL PRETEXTS TO WANT OF DILIGENCE.

"This way."

Evie's eye skipped to the bottom of the page,

where B. L. Lynch had signed his name.

"Let's go now. This way."

The older man was standing to one side, staring at her. His eyes flickered past her to the front door. One of the younger men stood quickly and went to stand in front of it. The older man took Evie's forearm in a tight grip and pulled her forward.

The stairs seemed endless as he guided her downward. At the bottom, he turned her sharply to the right and lifted a latch bar with his free hand. Quickly, he swung her forward as he opened the door. The instant she was inside, the door was shut and she could hear the latch dropping back into place before she had time to react at all.

"Who's there?"

It was Pa's voice in the darkness, steady and even like it always was.

"Me," Evie said, her voice failing in her dry throat, shrinking to a whisper. "I'm here, Pa. I have the papers."

"Oh, thank God," Mama whispered, and Evie came forward, her arms outstretched, until she found her mother in the impossible darkness of the slave pen. Her mother was already crying, and Evie felt the tears that she had held off all day rising to flood her own eyes.

"You have all the papers?" Pa asked.

"Yes," Evie told them. "Ours and yours, too, Mama."

"Thank God," Mama said again, and Pa echoed her. Then they stood in a circle, swaying and hugging, for a long time before they lay down on the dirt floor and slept.

When I reread yesterday's entry, it is hard to believe that so much could have happened to us since then.

At Lynch's this morning, it was just like Pa said it would be. They would have sold us South if they could have. But Willis Jackson had told Pa what to do if he ever was in danger like that, and Pa explained it to Mama and me. Willis said it couldn't fail and none of us had a better idea, so we did it. We waited until they marched us into the selling hall and had men standing all around, maybe twenty or more. They had bids on us, and we waited until they were done and one man actually thought he had bought Pa and another me and Mama. Then I pulled out the papers and Pa and Mama and I, all three, held them up so that all the men in the room could see. I was shaking all over. Mama was crying. Pa was the only one who believed it would really work. He said it had to with that many men in the room. "All it takes is one honest man and none of the others will dare try to take the papers away," Pa said. "And there will be many more than one honest man." And I guess it was so. They let us go soon after that, apologizing a little as they led us down the halls to a back door on the alley.

We walked home. I told Pa about everything on the way—about the Maloney brothers and Terrence's good heart and how afraid I was of Mr. Maloney making trouble for him, and for us. We weren't home thirty minutes before Terrence came over, all shy and quiet. Mama washed his cuts for him and he was following her around like a puppy before morning had passed. His ma is a nice woman, I think, but is worked so hard, she has no time to be soft. Mama says she is going to call upon her one day when we know her Mister is gone for a while. Mama says sometimes women can work these things out better than men. Not always, but sometimes. I hope so.

Fiona came by after school. Mama thinks she is adorable with her red braids and her freckles. Fiona said, "Why didn't you ever tell me your mother is so nice?" She said it with Mama standing there so of course Mama had to puff up and tease me about not bragging about her when I should.

Fiona told me later—when we were outside—that Liam and Sean got hollered at for all the trouble they caused Lynch's men. I am glad. They deserved it and more. Fiona stayed for a while and we brushed the mares while we talked. Ginger likes Fiona because she brings her pieces of carrot sometimes. Terrence had put them in their stalls backward last night— with Ginger in Lucky's stall and Lucky in Ginger's— but besides that, he did a perfect job. They had hay and water and he hung up the harness. Pa thanked him and gave him a nickel and he blushed. His poor face looks so sore. I can't imagine why a grown man would hit a boy like that. Pa says there is no end to the badness and the goodness in the world. I suppose he is right.

Pa made another hiding place this evening. We put Mama's papers there, and ours in the old one. Just in case, Pa says. When we were walking home this morning, all of us stiff and tired and hungry, we started talking about going West. I think Mama might just think about it now. Maybe, anyway. I never thought we would. Pa wants to go to California. Mama said Oregon sounds better to her. We had to laugh. They don't either one know anything much about either place. I guess after a night at Lynch's, any place sounds better than here. Maybe we won't feel like that tomorrow.

Well, I am tired and my candle is about to gutter, so I will fill more of this page tomorrow. Thank you, God, for getting us home and keeping us together. Look out for Terrence, please, and don't let his brothers pick on him so much.

Oh, I almost forgot . . .

Pa whispered to me at bedtime that we would give Mama her sewing machine tomorrow. It'll be like a dozen Christmastimes for her. I can't wait to see her smile.

AMERICAN *Diaries*

by Kathleen Duey

EXPERIENCE ALL THE
American Diaries ADVENTURES!

#1 Sarah Anne Hartford

#2 Emma Eileen Grove

#3 Anisett Lundberg

#4 Mary Alice Peale

#5 Willow Chase

#6 Ellen Elizabeth Hawkins

#7 Alexia Ellery Finsdale

#9 Celou Sudden Shout

#10 Summer MacCleary

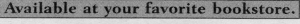

Available at your favorite bookstore.

❧ ALADDIN PAPERBACKS
An imprint of Simon & Schuster Children's Publishing Division